I0553542

The Time Chair Diary

Book Two

UNDERGROUND

By Laura Crockett

WOMAN WITH A PAST PRODUCTIONS

A subsidiary of

Historical Resources Publishing

The Time Chair Diary, Book Two, Underground
Copyright©2017 Laura Crockett

Cover artwork by Zimke Zolvoljni

ISBN: 0-9785713-2-0

WOMAN WITH A PAST PRODUCTIONS

A subsidiary of

Historical Resources Publishing

www.historicalresourcespublishing.com

To my grandson,
Malcolm.

Prologue

From Book One,
Big Battles in Trenton

"Does that mean I get to go again?" I said.

"If you want." The Old Man stood up and turned toward the center of the warehouse. He was waiting. He pulled out a pocket watch from his pants pocket to check the time. His lips moved. He was counting the seconds backwards. When he reached the number one, the time chair appeared. The fog cleared, the glass came up, and the dog that had chased me jumped out of the chair.

"That dog again!" The dog barked at the Old Man. "Plato!" I yelled out, holding a piece of bacon in my hand. Plato then turned to me to bark. "Plato, shshsh!" I threw the bacon at him. He stopped to eat. A second piece of bacon kept him from barking again. By the time I threw a third piece, he was wagging his tail. In minutes, he was my long, lost friend.

"Looks like you got yourself a dog."

"Don't we have to send him back?"

"Not just now." The Old Man removed the clock from its slot in the back of the time machine. "I have to visit my grandmother," he continued as he walked into the front office. In a moment, he returned carrying another clock, which he placed into the slot.

"Your grandmother is still alive?"

"No, she's not here." He slid open the number seven door to grab a coat and scarf. "She's there," he said, motioning with his head toward the time chair. He placed a bowler hat on his head. "I like seeing her as a young woman. She thinks of me as just another boarder in her boarding house. Her cooking is so good, well," he patted his belly, "it's a weakness I have." He jumped onto the chair.

"I thought you were too old for time travel?"

"Not when it concerns the heart." He said it gently. "Or my stomach."

"But what do I do now?"

"Hang the uniform in the closet and lock the door on your way out." As the glass came down, he wrapped the scarf around his neck. The engine started to hum, the fog came, the lights flashed, and he was gone.

Suddenly, the warehouse seemed so very lonely. I gave Plato a petting, and then changed back into my own clothes. Plato followed me into the office from the warehouse. "Hmm, what am I to do with you?" Plato wagged his tail. "Well, boy, I guess it's you and me because who knows when anyone will come back. Come on, boy."

No sooner had I opened the door than I heard the time chair's engine humming. I returned to the warehouse to see who it was. When the fog cleared and the glass lifted, a young black man stumbled out. He was dressed in overalls and an old shirt, with a red scarf tied around his neck. On his head was a big straw hat. He looked frightened when he saw me. Plato barked.

"Who are you?" he asked. "Where is Moses?" He looked around the warehouse.

"Who is Moses? Where are you from? You don't look ancient to me."

"I am looking for Harriet Tubman. Moses."

"What year is it?"

"1854."

Then I remembered. Harriet Tubman was the woman who organized the Underground Railroad. "That Mrs. Tubman?" I said questioning myself as much as the young man.

"It was dark. I asked him about Moses. He told me to go hide in the orchard."

Prologue

"He? Who?"

"That fat man, older, a free black, I think. Working with Mrs. Tubman, I think. I went to the orchard, then stumbled, fell into that *thing*. Then lights flashed, the glass came down. I was trapped! What is that thing?"

For a moment, I was speechless, staring back at the young man who waited for my answer.

"That thing..." I began.

Chapter One

Lamentations

"Where are you from?" I waited for an answer.

He eyed Plato. "I'm not sayin'."

I detected a Southern accent. Plato didn't move.

"My name's Ell. What's yours?"

"I'm called Lamentations."

"That sounds Biblical."

"It is." He looked around the warehouse as he spoke. His eyes came back to Plato. Neither moved.

"Where did you find the, ah, chair?"

"Like I told you. In the orchard." Keeping his eyes on Plato, he started to cross to the windows on the east side.

"Wait!"

He stopped.

"You're someplace you shouldn't be." I positioned myself between him and the windows. "It wouldn't be a good idea for you to look out those windows."

His eyes narrowed. He looked at me, and then up towards the windows. "What's out there?" His face showed he was thinking. Then he said, "Slavers?" He pointed with his chin. "Out there? I reached the safe place?" He looked back to me.

I didn't know what he was talking about. What did he mean by "slavers" and "safe places?"

"That's alright, then. I won't look out and let myself be seen." He sat at the table, in the chair Martin had sat in. "I'll wait."

I sighed in relief. Plato laid down on the rug in front of the office door as if it was now his duty, to guard the office. He seemed used to the warehouse, as though he belonged.

"You got yourself a nice huntin' dog there. Belong to your brother?"

"My brother?" I turned to look at the dog. "He belongs to me, I guess. Or at least now he does."

Lamentations looked at me quizzically. "Someone give him to you?"

"You could say that, yes." I searched for something to say while I prayed for the Old Man or Martin to come back to the warehouse. In the silence, I could hear the clocks ticking in the front office even with the door closed. I think he did as well because he stared at the office door. What I wanted was to tell him about the chair. The Old Man's rules forbade that. He sure was adamant about those rules. However, he would have to bend a little, because this guy had made the trip *here*, and he would need to go *back there*. Wherever "back there" was.

I studied the way he was dressed. He wore an off white blouse type shirt under overalls that were well worn at the knees. He had removed his large brimmed straw hat and placed it on the table. Now he untied the red kerchief from around his neck to wipe his forehead. He was worried. Something weighed on his mind besides having fallen into a strange chair that had taken him to a girl and a dog in a warehouse on South Clinton Street in Trenton. I took the chair opposite him.

"Look, Mr. Lamentations, it's tricky, see, I mean about what's happened to you because, well, I can't say."

"You are a confusing child." He rubbed his hands with his kerchief.

"I don't mean to be." I took a deep breath. "Please, be patient with me."

"Lamentations is always a patient man."

My smile to him was weak. With all the thinking I was doing, I still had not come up with a solution. Nor could I think of a good lie to tell him. Then it struck me that I should look at the dials on the time chair because those dials would tell me where that chair had been, and when it had been.

"Excuse me," I said as I got up to go to the chair. Lamentations' eyes followed me as I crossed over to it. I peered at the dials. It read "1854." I looked back at Lamentations. "The year is 1854!"

"Yes, did I not tell you that?"

"October."

Lamentations stood. "What's this about?" He started to cross to me. "Why is the year important?"

"Mr. Lamentations, sir, I have to get you back."

"Back?" He now stood next to me. He peered in at the dials. "Yes, what are those funny lookin' clocks for?"

"Sir, I know I'm supposed to answer questions when adults ask, but I can't do that."

"Not when a slave ask, that's for certain."

"A what?"

Slavery was something we read about in school. It was like all the rest of history presented in the books. Flat and lifeless. Just a fact of the past, and that past had nothing to do with us. Or so we like to think. As a kid, what was I supposed to know about the far reaching effects of our past immoralities as a nation? Now, without asking about it, I was confronted by a piece of history I had rarely thought about. Well, girl, I told myself, you want to know everything, here's your chance to know something not so glorious.

But hold on, I said to myself. The Old Man isn't here to arrange the travel. Besides, the history I knew about slavery and the runaways, which I thought this man must be, was limited. I had not read any extra books on it, nor had it fired my imagination in any way. Yet, when I was a small child, Martin Luther King had been murdered and there had been terrible riots in Trenton right after that. That too I had not pondered.

Still, the conversation inside my heard continued, and it started to repeat itself about how this man was *here*. And he needed to get *back there*. I could see he was already sweating from the Trenton summer heat, so pretty soon he would figure out he was no longer in October. I recalled how the Old Man had worn a jacket and a scarf when he had left on the chair. Somehow Lamentations had found the chair after the Old Man left it. Then where had Professor Clawson gone? What city? Must be Trenton.

"Drat!" I said out loud.

"What was that?"

"Serves me right for not having studied this more at the library."

"Yes, child, if you say so."

"Of course I could get to the library and back...."

Lamentations narrowed his eyes again in scrutiny of my face. I turned away. My bike was outside. I could get to the library in a matter of minutes, but it might take me hours to study up on everything I needed to know. A second thought jumped in. Perhaps I could call Jersey Jones, a black kid I knew from summer camp. Nah, he would start asking questions that couldn't be answered.

Oh yes, I was in a pickle. But if I waited much longer to act, there could be hell to pay for it. I walked over to the wardrobe, opened doors until I found the closet with the 19th century marked on it.

"You have a lot of clothes there. Must be a rich girl."

"No sir." I looked back at him. "Well, maybe you're right. But not in the way you might think."

Lamentations had that look on his face again. Thinking back on it, this man must have been horribly confused as well as frightened. Yet he didn't show it. He was a man in command of his emotions, something I was too young to grasp. Or appreciate. It was that command that would save us later.

"I don't know what to wear."

"Your family know you dress like a field hand?"

"What?" I looked down at my clothes. I still had on my plaid shirt and bluejeans. "Oh," I said with a smile. "No," I lied in the cause of keeping the rules of time travel. "That's why I have to change, you see, because that chair there," I motioned toward the time chair, "That has a machine that will take me and you back to the orchard, then I have to go home." I spoke slowly so that I would recall every lie, if needed, later on. The going back home part was not a lie. I wanted to be home in the worst way, so I could be rid of this problem that confronted me in the person of this man called Lamentations.

"Wear that," he said pointing, his kerchief in his hand.

I looked down at the dress I had pulled out. It was a dark blue dress, with a wide skirt, with ruffles along the bottom of the skirt that led up to the waist. Tied around the top of the hanger was a white petticoat that was hooped. There was also a straw hat, with matching dark blue ribbon around its crown. At the end of the long sleeves there was a white lace ruffle. It looked complicated, but more than that, it looked like it would be a warm outfit to wear. Then I recalled I would be going back to fall weather, so the decision was made. This dress would do, especially since Lamentations said it would.

"I'll be right back." I ran toward the bathroom. Then I remembered: Lamentations must not look out those windows while I was gone. I halted.

"You're not goin' to leave me alone with that dog, are you?"

My mind worked quickly. He was afraid of the dog. I slowly turned toward Plato.

"Plato, go over there," I said as I pointed toward the windows. Plato understood. He obeyed. "Mr. Lamentations sir, promise me you will not look out those windows."

Lamentations glanced at Plato who now sat quietly under the windows. "I don't go over there, no."

I left the room. In the bathroom it took me awhile to figure out how to put on that outfit. When I was reasonably dressed, I returned to the warehouse. Lamentations, when he saw me, gasped audibly, then turned his head so as not to look at me.

"Child, you must finish dressing."

"What?" I looked down. My legs were bare. "I'll get some shoes from the shoe drawer," I said as I pulled out the drawer marked "Shoes." I found it full of bootie type shoes. I tried on a tan pair that looked to fit. They were a little too small. Remembering how the too large eighteenth century shoes had hurt my feet, and with my blisters still evident, I pawed through the drawer again to see if I couldn't come up with a better fitting pair. I tried on a dark brown pair that fit me well. Now I needed stockings. I spied a basket at the bottom of the closet. It was full of stockings plus bloomers. I realized this may have been what Lamentations had been referring to. Back to the bathroom I went. Minutes later, now fully dressed, and already feeling uncomfortable, I returned to find Lamentations had not moved, nor had Plato.

"Well, Mr. Lamentations, am I alright now?"

He turned to look at me. "You look nice, young lady. Put on your hat and we best get goin' 'cause this place is too strange for Lamentations."

"Wait," I said. I looked around. Where was my watch? I ran back to the closet, reached in to my uniform coat pocket. Right where I had left it. I grabbed it, then looked for a purse. I found one. I shoved the watch into the purse. "Come on, then," I said as I jumped into the chair.

Lamentations hesitated when he approached.

"It's alright. It will be tight, but we'll fit. Come on." I padded the seat next to me. "Believe me, I don't have any cooties."

"Cooties?" Lamentations slid in beside me.

I was too busy paying attention to the dials to answer. The year already indicated 1854. The return dial was set to 1974. I left the location dials and switches as they were. I remembered that to leave the warehouse, the Old Man had pressed the red switch down. I pressed it. The hiss sounded. The glass doors started to come down. Lamentations stiffened. His eyes grew wide.

"It's alright. We are getting you back to where you belong." I leaned back in anticipation of the jolt that would knock us out. Plato began to bark. He came around to my side of the chair. Just before the glass came all the way down, he quickly crawled in and lay flat on the floor. Now Lamentation was really scared. But only his face showed it. He stayed as still as could be. The glass sealed, the motor whirred, the fog began to envelop us. Lamentations took deep breaths and Plato howled. The bright lights flashed their colors and then the blackness came.

Chapter Two

The Orchard

"This thing is the devil, I tell you!"

Lamentations seethed. He twisted to the right. He wanted out. The glass then hissed, the clouds dissipated. It was night outside. Lamentations, breathing in shallow bursts, strained to see what was through the clouds. I wanted to tell him, to explain it so that he wouldn't be frightened. The rules of time travel didn't allow for that. My secret burdened me.

"You can get out in just a minute. As soon as the glass lifts all the way." Plato stood up in anticipation. After two trips, he knew what to expect. It wouldn't do for him to get out because I didn't want to be in 1854 for more than a few minutes, just long enough to send Lamentations on his way. Once he was gone, and could no longer see the time chair, I would return to the warehouse. Then Plato dashed out barking at something.

"Plato!"

"Where's he going?"

Before I could reply, Lamentations ducked out as well. I could hear his footsteps-the fog had yet to be completely cleared-as he ran across the ground. That was a relief, that we were on solid ground. I sighed, thinking I should just leave Plato in 1854. Someone would take him in as he was a beaut of a hunting dog. Nonetheless, that would not be responsible. How could I know what havoc that dog could wreak in the time continuum? With an even deeper sigh, I turned my body to jump out of the machine.

I could make out that we had landed in the middle of a great many trees. That meant the chair would be somewhat hidden. My feet hit the ground. Then I heard something that sounded like a car crash.

"More of the devil's doing!" Lamentations shouted out.

Now I had to be quick! Fighting to see what was beyond the clouds, I ran in the direction of the crash. In seconds I found myself headed down an alleyway. It led to a street; yes a street, not a dirt road, but a paved one in downtown Trenton. In 1854? There were electric street lights, a cement sidewalk and to my right was a car all right, that had hit a light pole. The driver leaned against the steering wheel. I hesitated. What if he was dead? No time for wondering. I ran over to check his pulse. He was alive. I stepped back from the car. It was an old Model T. It was my turn to be frightened because something had gone wrong. Seriously wrong. I glanced around. Lamentations stood in the shadows of the alleyway. Plato sat on the other side of the street.

"Blasted dog!" The man in the car had come to.

"Plato," I whispered. "Plato, you changed something." I started to run across the street toward the dog. "This can't be!"

Plato saw me coming. He knew he had done something he wasn't supposed to do. He lowered his head in shame.

"He ran across the road and that thing turned out of the way to avoid hitting him. Hit that light pole instead." Lamentations stared up at the light. He pointed to it. "That thing doesn't flicker."

I ran back across the street, Plato following me.

"Lamentations, we've got to go back."

"Go back? Go back where?" He glanced up the alleyway. "Not in that thing again. No miss. Never again for Lamentations." He backed away.

"Mr. Lamentations, something is wrong, we have to go back!" I grabbed hold of his sleeve.

"I *not* ride in that thing no more."

The driver got out of the car. "Look at my car." He looked over at Plato. "I oughta shoot that dog!" He then turned to point at Lamentations. " And that nigger too." He walked toward Lamentations.

Plato had no collar for me to grab hold of, so I grabbed him by the fur of his neck. "Come on Plato, get to the chair." Plato stood. But instead of obeying me he began to bark at the driver of the car. I didn't know what to do. Lamentations looked to run away.

"Please sir, " I cried out, "I'll take my dog back home."

The man stopped. He turned his glare from Lamentations to me. "Who are you? Who are your parents? And what are you doing out here at this time of night?"

I had no idea about the time except that it was dark. As with all time travel, a traveler has to think on her feet when the occasion calls for it.

"Came out looking for my dog, mister."

"Well you found him. Now you tell me, whose going to pay for that?" He pointed to his car.

I swallowed hard. "I guess I will."

"*You* will?" He eyed me closely. "Where have you been? To a fancy dress party?" His anger seemed to cool somewhat. "Guess your parents have money. Where do you live? Princeton?"

"Please, sir, this is just a girl. No need talkin' to her about it."

While the man had been talking to me, Lamentations had inched closer.

"You shut your mouth boy, until I ask you a question." The man's tone changed. That's what scared me about him because Lamentations was a large man. The driver of the car was thin and rather short. Yet he was not afraid of Lamentations. Lamentations, however, was afraid of him.

"Mister," I said, "if you write down your telephone number, my parents will call you first thing in the morning. I promise."

The driver reached into his pocket and removed a business card. This he held out to me. "Take it. And now you better tell me your name, and the name of your servant here. And that dog. What are you doing with that dog out here at night?"

"Part of my costume, sir. That's all. And my name is Ell, Ell Evans."

"What kind of name is Ell?"

"Ell, first name is really Laura. But I don't like being called that. So I use the first initial."

"You relations with Bob Evans?"

That was my grandfather's name, but I decided to lie. "He's my uncle. You can talk to him." I took hold of Lamentations' sleeve. I pulled him toward the alley.

"Really, we have to go now. My parents are waiting for us." I turned to march resolutely up the alley. "Come on, Mr. Lamentations," I whispered.

"Just a minute here. You haven't given me your parents' name or telephone number."

The alley was dark. "Let's run!" And run I did, with Lamentations following close behind me. Plato ran ahead of us. He too sensed the urgency of the moment.

"Hey!" We heard the man yelling. "Get back here, the both of you!"

We ran harder. I had no idea of where we were, but thought we might be near the Assunpink Creek because I heard water running. Somehow, I needed to figure out a way to double back to the orchard, but now we heard footsteps, at the run, following us. Someone blew a whistle. Police!

"There, just ahead!" a man's voice shouted.

"This way," whispered Lamentations as he pulled me to the left. We ran past a dark house. The alleyway turned to dirt. The sound of the water grew louder. I was afraid we would end up over the steep edge of the creek. Lamentations, however, stopped us in time. He surveyed the embankment, and then jumped down to land by the creek. "Give me your hands!" he said as he lifted his arms to me. I took hold and he swung me down to stand next to him. He stepped into the shadows of the embankment. I did too. Where Plato was I could only guess.

"You see where they went?" a man's voice said above us.

"No," another man replied. "Listen, Harry, you said there was a girl in a fancy costume with a negro?"

"That's what I said." It was Harry speaking.

"They could've fallen over the edge on a night like tonight."

"We would have heard screams, or a splash. Nah, that girl knows people here in town. She's been let into a house." It was another man's voice.

A few moments of silence followed, an absolute stillness with nothing but the sound of the creek filling the night. Then the policeman spoke.

"Harry, go home. We'll look into it in the morning."

His voice came from right near the edge of the embankment.

"Yes, well, I guess. But you call me first thing."

"I will. Now go home and get some sleep. We'll have the car towed to your house."

We waited. When we could no longer hear any footsteps, we waited some more.

"What do you think?" I whispered.

"I think we crawl out of here."

Lamentations walked downstream a bit until he found a dip in the embankment that allowed us to crawl up it. When we stood on the dirt again, I got a sense of my whereabouts. I pointed to the left. "That's the way to the orchard."

"I ain't goin' back there, miss, no. Lamentations will find his own way out of town."

"Lamentations, you cannot stay here. You hear me? You *cannot stay here.*"

"I will not go back with you to sit in that devil's machine. Or git myself into any more crazy things like that carriage with no horses. Another devil's machine, if you ask me."

"I don't ask you. I tell you." I reached up to his face and forced him to look at me. "You're a slave, so now I will give you an order. You hear me?"

"You ain't my owner."

"But I could find him."

Lamentations paused, then said slowly, "I don't think you would."

"Don't test me."

Lamentations stared at me for what seemed like forever. He stepped away from me.

"In the morning those policemen will look for you."

"They look for you, too," he said.

"If they see you they will grab you hoping to find me. Because they think you are my servant. But I won't be here. I'll be back there." I jerked my head back.

"You talkin' in those riddles again."

"You have to trust me." I begged.

He stopped. He was thinking. I was too. How much did I need to tell him to get him back into that chair? That was my dilemma. Whether I lied or told the truth, it did not matter. Getting him back into that chair did. Lamentations must be returned to his timeline.

"You have to trust me," I repeated. "You know, don't you, deep inside, you cannot be here. In Trenton."

"In Trenton?" He paused.

"Please, Mr. Lamentations."

After a moment he said, "Nobody called me a slave." He said it to himself as much as he said it to me.

"What do you mean?" In my gut, I knew what he meant, but I didn't want to say it out loud or inside my head.

"Somehow, they way I figurin' this, I am in the years yet to come. Or I am in a dream."

I kept my silence. Lamentations looked down at me. I had never seen a man think so hard. He crouched down to the ground, folded his hands in front of him.

"That's it, ain't it. Yes, Miss Ell, you can't say, but that's it. This ain't a dream. Lamentations is wide awake. Don't trouble your head none, I won't try to get you to disobey whoever it was made the rule." He looked at me and smiled. "Now I got some figurin' to do. Because if I don't go back, my sister will be in slavery for the rest of her life. And that mean I break my promise to our mother. So Lamentations, he has to obey you, and ride the devil once again."

"Where is your sister?"

"Still in Maryland. But she is given over to her master's daughter who is fixin' to marry someone from Georgia. I'll never see that girl again if I don't get Mrs. Tubman to bring her out."

I had heard a little about Mrs. Tubman, but not enough to understand the circumstances I was presented with.

"And your mother?" I asked.

"Dead. She died last month. That's when I made my way out of Maryland." He leaned back on his haunches. "Marini was already livin' with Miss Lavinia, in the house, so I couldn't bring her out with me. That's why I got to find this Mrs. Tubman."

I nodded. "We won't find her here." I held out my hand to him. He took it, stood, and together, we walked along the Assunpink until we came to the edge of the orchard. Here, it was exceptionally dark. We made our way through it, tree to tree. Finally, I could see the outline of the chair. I breathed a sound of relief. I fingered in my small purse for the watch. It was there. I took it out, but it was too dark to read the time. The little red light blinked steadily. Then, near the chair, something moved. We stopped, each of us stepping behind a tree. It was Plato. I was, once more, relieved.

To the East the dawn presented itself. I grabbed hold of Lamentations' arm to pull him toward the chair. He balked.

"We have to leave here, now, Mr. Lamentations. We have to." I tugged on his arm. He nodded. He understood but he didn't like it. Nor did I. Whatever had gone wrong to get us to Trenton, that something could happen again. But Trenton was no place for either of us, or Plato. I took hold of the watch and pressed it. The glass raised up. We climbed inside. The destination dial had changed. It said 1924. I set it to 1854, checking it twice to make certain I had it right. Next I checked the location. Everything seemed correct. I pressed the switch to begin the operation. The glass came down. The hum of the engine was a welcome sound. Soon came the fog, the whining, the lights,, and then the black out.

Chapter Three

1854

The chair settled. The lights dimmed. The whine gave way to the hiss. The glass lifted. Lamentations rolled out onto the ground. He softly groaned. Plato landed beside him. I waited for a minute. I wanted to be sure. Of what, I don't know. The times when I would bound out of the chair were over for me. I had learned a bit of patience. An eleven year old with a bit of patience is a thing to behold.

When all was quiet and still, I slowly swung my legs out to touch the ground. It felt firm. I leaned in to check the dials. It said 1854, and that it was October 20. The location read 39.95 by 76.16. I had no idea what that meant. I stood. I looked around. The sun was setting in the West. Turning south, I could see the outlines of buildings in the distance. Behind me were trees. To my left, the Delaware River.

Lamentations stood up. He pointed toward the buildings. "That is Philadelphia." He then started walking.

"Lamentations!" It was a hearty whisper. He paused, turned to face me.

"Let's go."

I hesitated. My gut feeling was to turn around, get onto the chair and return to 1974 in Trenton. My heart, however, wanted to follow. Here was my chance, as the Old Man put it, to experience, to feel, history. Shall we experience? I asked. I was dressed for it, but not prepared mentally. I knew so little of this era, for I had not read the dozens of books on it as I had on the American War for Independence. My brain told me I should stay here.

"I can't go with you." I smiled but he could not see it.

"I understand. You got me back, that's all I can ask."

"Good luck with your sister. I hope you find her."

"First, gotta find Moses. No Moses, no promised land." Lamentations turned away and then headed toward the city.

Plato stood still, smelling the air. His tail wagged. He looked at me. He wanted a command of some sort.

"Come on, boy, we need to get back."

Plato's ears perked up, but not at me. He looked beyond, to the chair. I glanced back. The engine began its whine. When the hiss started I dashed to the chair. My watch lay on the seat. I dove under the glass just in time. But instead of the glass coming all the way down, it stopped. The chair shuddered. The watch bounced onto the floor. I reached down and grabbed it. The red light on the watch was out. I shook it gently. It did not come back on. I wound it up. It stayed off. The chair was extremely quiet; and too motionless. The dials were not lit up. I touched them, moved the switches up and down. No response of any kind.

"Well, Plato, it looks like we will be here after all." I got out of the chair. "Come on boy, we best go with Lamentations." I stroked the dog's head. "The Old Man will figure it out." I took a deep breath. "I hope." It was getting dark. Lamentations' shadow of a figure was barely visible. "Come on Plato!" We both moved forward at a run. Then, after several yards, I heard the familiar whining. I stopped to look back just in time to see the chair disappear into time. "Got to be the Old Man." I stood motionless. I wanted to cry I felt so alone. Instead, I took a deep breath as I hoped for the best. It was my second stoic moment during time travel. By now it did seem to me that when time traveling, one had to be prepared for malfunctions.

For now, there was nothing more to do but to catch up to Lamentations. Plato came in handy. He sniffed the ground as we walked. I trusted him. Don't ask why. It was a gut feeling I had towards him. Though he had an owner back in the eighteenth century, I felt he now belonged to me. Or we belonged together.

We reached a road that led into the city. Plato kept his nose down and we went straight into the outskirts where there were a few buildings. The more we advanced, the more buildings were along the road. We passed a blacksmith who stoked his fire. He was a black man. I walked over to him hoping he had seen Lamentations.

"Excuse me, sir."

"Are you lost, miss?" he responded.

"Why yes I am. I am looking for a friend of mine. A black man. I wonder if you have seen him?"

"You will have to give me a little more to go on than that." He looked up, out at the street.

I turned in the direction he faced. There were many black men and black women and children on the road.

"Oh." I turned back to him. "Where is this place?"

"Colored Town, Philadelphia."

"He's wearing overalls, a white shirt, a straw hat on his head, and a red kerchief is tired around his neck."

"Haven't seen him, miss. Can I give you directions to the center of Philadelphia?"

"No thank you. It is important that I find him."

"Tell you what. Why don't you head on down this road and you will find shops and such. Perhaps he stopped into a shop. If he does happen by, can I give him a message?"

"Tell him Miss Ell and Plato are looking for him."

The blacksmith looked over at Plato. "Plato the dog?" I nodded. "Fine dog."

"Thank you." I smiled weakly. The blacksmith nodded in reply.

"Come on boy, we'll find him."

Just as the blacksmith had said, we soon found ourselves in a busy section of town. It was filled with shops of all sorts, most of them closing for the evening. Two horses approached from the opposite direction, rather faster than they should have. Plato barked at them.

"Shut that dog up!" a voice loud with command bent down to me. I glanced up. The voice belonged to a man who seemed square in his build. His hands were large, his face full of tense muscles, his cheek bones high. His hair was a dark tumble of curls carelessly hanging over his broad forehead. His hat was pushed to the back of his head. He had bushy brows that were reddish brown. The nose was long, ending in a well formed point between his nostrils. "Did ya hear me, girl? Shut him up, or my man will." The square man had an Irish accent.

"Plato!" He came to my side but growled steadily at the man.

"Mr. Gannon!" cried out another's man's voice. The square man acknowledged the voice that called out his name.

"You are?" Mr. Gannon said as he turned away from me.

The man who called out was a rather small man, with a firm but kind face. He wore a dark suit. His boots were muddied. He stepped onto the road. He approached Mr. Gannon. "These are free blacks, sir, and your presence here is unsettling."

"Where I come from, sir, there are no free negroes, none at all." He sneered as he glanced around.

"No, I reckon not. But you are in Philadelphia now, and unless-" The small man stopped speaking as soon as he saw me. "Here, who is this young lady?"

Gannon turned back towards me. "No idea." He looked straight at me. "You there, with that cur, who are you?"

"Me? No one." I took hold of Plato's neck, wishing he had a collar. Plato pushed himself against me. He kept growling.

"She's obviously a young lady, sir. Mind your talk."

The black suited one came around Gannon's horse. Plato stiffened. "Stay!" I hissed down at him. He obeyed.

"Excuse me miss, I am Seth Peterson. Are you lost?"

"Well sir, I believe I am."

"And you are?"

"I'm-" I began to say "Ell" but instead used my real given name. "I'm Laura. Laura Evans." I said it quietly as I didn't want that Gannon man to know my name.

"If you will allow me, Miss Evans, I will escort you and your Springer to the sidewalk." He held out his arm to me. Plato stopped growling. The three of us walked across the street. "Mrs. Bishop!" he called out when we got to the sidewalk. A large black woman wearing a dark blue dress with a starched apron came out of a shop. "Mrs. Bishop, please be so kind as to keep this young lady in your premises until I can escort her home."

"Yes, of course, Mr. Peterson."

From the shop window I watched with Mrs. Bishop as Mr. Peterson paused on the sidewalk to write a note. This he gave to a young black man who ran quickly down the street with it. I glanced around the street itself. It was just as the blacksmith had said. This was Colored Town, for there were blacks everywhere. I turned to Mrs. Bishop.

Without hearing my question, she answered it.

"Free blacks live in this neighborhood," she said to me. "So men like this Gannon come here looking for runaways."

"Runaways?"

"Yes." Mrs. Bishop looked down at me. "Where are you from?"

"New Jersey."

"You're a ways from home."

"I'm visiting."

Just then, Mr. Gannon's assistant, a dark skinned young man, with refined features, removed a brown, leather book from his saddle bag. This he handed to Mr. Gannon.

Mrs. Bishop pointed to the assistant with her chin. "He is mixed, that one, son of his white master and African mother."

"What do you mean?"

Well, dear child, you are a northern girl, and not used to the realities that coloreds face. You are young, and I won't say anything further." She turned her attention back to the scene in the street.

"What's that book?"

"That's his book of runaways. He's got pictures and writings that tell him what each one look like. Even more than the drawings do, every little mole, birthmark or scar makes its way into that book. Yes, little one, that assistant of his is bad, but Gannon is the very devil himself, to us."

"He speaks harshly."

Mrs. Bishop nodded her head. "I don't think he has a kind word for anyone. He handles those he catches more harshly than his words. You do not want to cross him, no you do not!" Mrs. Bishop backed away from the window. "Stay away, far away, from the likes of him." She picked up the broom. "How did you end up on our street? A white girl like you?"

"It's a long story."

"Until the police come, Mr. Peterson will not leave here. We got time," Mrs. Bishop swept her shop. "You say you are visiting?"

"I am here looking for someone. I got lost, took a wrong turn." I looked around the shop as I spoke. It was what we would call a candle shop. The shelves were lined with candles, candle sticks, table candelabras and hurricane glasses. From the ceiling hung chandeliers made from all sorts of materials; brass, cast iron and there was a small one of crystal that hung from the center rafter of the shop.

"You say you are from New Jersey?"

"Yes ma'am."

"Whereabouts?"

"Trenton."

"Trenton? What are you doing here? Your folks here or you staying with relatives?"

"Well, yes, I am here to see my old family friend. My mother said I could, so she sent me with trusted friends, and my dog here, who also is trustworthy."

Mrs. Bishop chuckled. "That's a good dog that can worry Gannon." Mrs. Bishop smiled at Plato. "You then lost your escort?"

"Yes ma'am, that's the way it is." I smiled at her.

"No worries with Mr. Peterson helping you. He's a kind and gentle soul. A Quaker." Mrs. Bishop leaned down to sweep the dirt into her dustpan. "They are good to us. Never turn in a runaway. Wish I could say the same for some of my neighbors. But when you're hungry, money comes in handy. So a body is sold out."

"Betrayed?"

Mrs. Bishop nodded.

"This Mr. Gannon catches runaway slaves?"

"Yes."

The way she said that, "yes", gave me a chill down my back.

Back out on the street, Mr. Peterson continued to speak to Gannon. From Gannon's expression, it was plain as day that he wished Mr. Peterson would go away.

"Why do you think this Mr. Gannon stays talking to Mr. Peterson?"

"Humph, he's looking for someone. He knows an escaped slave can disappear, like ice into water, in this neighborhood. Must be an expensive piece of human merchandise for him to stay." Mrs. Bishop had a trace of bitterness in her voice. She stood. "I'll be out the back for a minute." She left through the pale curtains behind the counter.

I returned to watching the men in the street. I allowed my eyes to wander, to see if I could find Lamentations. Whenever Gannon or his assistant would move their horses I desperately searched for my reluctant time traveler. Gannon's assistant shied away from something. That's when I saw his friendly face, just briefly peering out of the shadows of an alley opposite. I gasped. "Plato, there he is."

"There's who?"

Mrs. Bishop had returned silently. I turned to face her. She narrowed her eyes at me, her jaw set firm. "There's who?" she repeated.

"No one in particular."

Mrs. Bishop came up to the window. She looked across to where I had been looking. Her face showed no emotion, but soon she stepped back. "If I blow out candles, Gannon will notice something is different." Mrs. Bishop spoke in a hush. "But you tell me now, child, being honest as though you pray, your family friend is a black man?"

"Yes." I kept myself to a whisper.

"He don't want to be seen by Gannon. No he don't." Mrs. Bishop stepped behind the counter. "You stay at that window, and keep watching Mr. Peterson and Gannon. Don't do anything different."

"Yes ma'am."

Mrs. Bishop then disappeared into the back room. I returned to watching the street, with Mr. Peterson still talking. Three policemen then arrived. One spoke to Mr. Peterson, who, after a short chat, nodding towards Mr. Gannon. Mr. Peterson then left the police to deal with Mr. Gannon and his assistant. By that time, a crowd had gathered around the two slave hunters. The younger man made note of it to his master, but Mr. Gannon had no fear. Mr. Peterson then walked into the shop.

"Well, young lady, methinks this situation will soon right itself. Then we can get you back to your family."

"Thank you, sir. But it's friends I am with."

"Friends?"

"Of my family."

"I see. And the city overwhelmed you and you got lost?"

"Exactly, sir."

"Surely you have the address where you are staying?"

My mind raced. "Seventeen Maple Street, sir." It was the address of my aunt and uncle. Whether or not their house existed in 1854 I had no idea. But I knew it to be an old house.

"Maple street, that is south of here, and quite a distance. But never mind that. My buggy is right in back. It won't take us more than 45 minutes or so." Mr. Peterson checked his watch. "It's half-past seven now." He then looked around the shop. "Has Mrs. Bishop gone out?" With the question he poked his head through the curtains. "Hmm, well, I'll leave her a note." He took a small case from his coat pocket. This held small sheets of paper and a small pencil. He removed a sheet of paper and the pencil. He then proceeded to write on it. Just then Mrs. Bishop walked in. "Ah, there you are."

"I found your friend, Miss Laura." She held aside the curtain and there stood Lamentations.

"Lamentations!" I ran into the back room, I was so happy to see him unharmed. I took hold of his hands in mine. "You're free, you-" and then realizing what I was saying I clammed up.

Lamentations had a funny look on his face. He looked me over, frowned a bit, but then smiled. "You look a bit different, Miss Ell, but I guess that jus the city lights playing tricks on me."

"I am happy you're safe, that that Mr. Gannon didn't see you."

Mrs. Bishop laid her hand on my shoulder. "It's fine, Miss Laura, he is safe here, no one will give him up."

"Best you finish closing up, Mrs. Bishop." Mr. Peterson pointed to a chair. I sat. Lamentations sat on a barrel. He then turned to Lamentations. "I am sorry I heard your name, but I shall pretend I did not. I shall direct you to the proper helpers, and you," he turned back to me, "need to return to your home."

"That is a problem, sir."

"A problem how?"

"She know what she saying, " Lamentations quipped in speaking to Mr. Peterson.

"I fail to see humor here, if that is what you mean?" Mr Peterson said.

"I don't mean disrespect, sir, but she cannot tell you exactly where her home is. But I can tell you she helped me, and got into a bit of trouble doing it."

"I see." Mr. Peterson looked at me.

"It's like this, sir, " Lamentations continued, "I need your help. I need to find Mrs. Tubman." Lamentations pulled a letter from a hidden pocket inside his overalls. "Here, take this letter, please, and give it to her."

He handed the letter to Mr. Peterson. Mr. Peterson took it, unfolded it and read it silently. Mrs. Bishop, when she walked through the curtained door, quietly removed her apron, folded it neatly, put on her hat and then stood by waiting for Mr. Peterson to finish. When he had, he refolded the letter and held it in his hand.

"You know the contents of this letter?" he said without looking at Lamentations.

"Yes, sir."

"Then tear it apart, to shreds. If Gannon, or any other slave hunter gets ahold of it, the end of your freedom is assured. And your sister will be removed far into Georgia." Mr. Peterson returned the letter to Lamentations. "Mrs. Bishop here will lend you her assistance in your pursuits. May God bless you." Mr. Peterson turned to me. "Now, what to do with you, Miss Laura?"

"I want to stay with Lamentations, sir."

"No, absolutely not. Gannon has seen you. We mustn't let him see you again. Because through you, he can then find this man." He looked to Lamentations.

"I can put her on the ferry to Trenton." Mrs. Bishop said.

"Won't your friends wonder about you, Miss, or was that a ruse? Speak up, girl, you are involved in a dangerous undertaking, and for all we know, you are a spy."

"Oh no sir."

"She ain't, no spy, sir, and that is the good Lord's truth." Lamentations stood up to his full height.

"What am I to make of you?" Mr. Peterson looked me over. "You are an unusual child. Precocious, certainly. Yet, something else. What, I cannot put my finger on. Nonetheless, you are in danger. And, you are a danger to others. You understand?" I nodded. "I will take you with me to someone who can put you up for the night. In the meantime, I will get word to the Trenton Meeting. They will find your parents. They must be worried."

"I'm sure of it, sir."

"Mrs. Bishop, we will leave first."

Mrs. Bishop nodded her head.

"Where you taking Miss Ell?" Lamentations asked.

"Never you mind. The less we all know, the better. Say your farewells."

"Good night Mrs. Bishop. Thank you for watching over me, and finding Lamentations."

"You do as Mr. Peterson says, you hear me child?"

"Yes ma'am, I will." I turned to Lamentations. "Please find your sister, and both of you be well." To the shock of all in that storeroom, I gave Lamentations a hug, but he would not put his arms around me to return that affection.

Mr. Peterson led me out back. He helped me up into the buggy. "Will the Springer follow or shall we tie him?"

"He'll follow."

Mr. Peterson then untied his horse, took the reins, and then climbed in beside me. With a cluck of his tongue the horse walked down the alley until we turned right onto the street. Now, it was mostly deserted. A few more clucks of the tongue and the horse broke into a trot. This pace we kept up while we made our way out of part of town wherein lived the free blacks.

"Mr. Peterson?"

"Yes, Miss?"

"Who is this Gannon?"

Mr. Peterson sighed deeply. "He is a slave hunter. A wicked man, he stops at nothing in search of his prey."

"But why is he here? I mean, there are no slaves in Pennsylvania."

"There are runaways here, Miss Laura."

"But I thought if they could get here, to a free state, they would be safe?"

"Not so. They must hide, until they can make their way to Canada. Until they reach Canada, the laws of our nation say they can be picked up and returned to their masters."

We had now turned north onto the road that led us to the countryside.

"I didn't know that about the law that says they can be picked up and returned to their masters." I stared out into the blackness of the night. When, I wondered, was I to learn this in my schooling? It was the first time I comprehended that my education was sorely limited. "That's a long way to go, isn't, to Canada?"

"It is indeed."

"How far? How many miles?"
"I'm not certain. Perhaps 450 miles?"

Imagining that distance awed me. "How do they get there?"

"Why, they walk it. Or, if fortunate, they have a wagon or a horse to ride. But walking means they can hide easily."

"Walking, 450 miles.." I said it more to myself than to Mr. Peterson. Sighing over the thought, I sank back into the seat. I was tired. My eyes would not stay open. Soon, a blessed sleep overcame me. I don't think Mr. Peterson minded it one bit. After all, he had much to sort out in his mind. The last thing heard before the sweet oblivion of sleep was him sighing deeply again, and again.

I dreamed. In my dream, I was in a thick fog where bright, colored lights flicked on and off, here and there. In front of me was a steadily blinking red light. I walked towards it. Then I heard the voice of the Old Man calling out to me. "Ell, Ell, " he said. My eyes searched for him, but he was only a voice. "Ell, where are you?" It seemed the Old Man was searching for me.

"Here! Over here!" I called out.

The Old Man stepped out of the fog. He looked at me strangely, as if he didn't recognize me. Without a word, he peered closely at my face.

"No." he said. He walked back into the fog, which then cleared away to reveal a night sky with all its stars. I felt that same feeling I had felt before. Aloneness.

Another voice then reached me. A woman's voice. "You can't do this," she said. "Stop him. Go back and stop him." I now searched for a body to that voice, but nothing came of it.

"Can't do this to whom?" I cried out. My voice fell onto the dark sky that surrounded me. "Can't do this to whom?"

From the distance, I heard barking. I turned toward the sound. And then from that vast landscape of the void out ran Plato. "Shsh!" I said. He continued to bark. He jumped up against my body, nearly knocking me over. I felt myself reaching for something to cling to.

I awoke. The buggy was bouncing over the road. The horse was in a full gallop and Plato was barking at something. I turned to see Mr. Peterson urging his horse on.

"Mr. Peterson!" I screamed out.

"Hold on!" was his only response.

I grabbed on to the sides of the buggy. A shot rang out. There was a yelp, and then Plato's barking ceased. I was petrified. No matter the price, I had to look back. I couldn't see Plato anywhere. I did see Gannon and his assistant gaining on us, galloping their horses hard. Up ahead was a farm house. Mr. Peterson guided the horse toward the gates of this farm. We would have to stop to open the gate. Gannon could catch up with us by then.

"Do you have a gun?"

Mr. Peterson looked my way as though I was crazy. But my dad had taught me to shoot. To survive, I was willing to defend.

Mr. Peterson pulled the hard breathing horse up to the gate. "Open it!" he said to me. I jumped out, found the latch, and pushed on it with all my might. It gave easily enough. Mr. Peterson's buggy was right behind me. When the buggy was clear enough, I started closing the gate. Gannon was now ten feet away from us. He shot point blank into the buggy. I yelled. The horse bolted up the drive. Someone from the farm house stepped out onto their porch. "Who goes?" he called out. Gannon lifted his rifle to fire. I reached down to hopefully grab a rock, or anything to throw. I got lucky. I found a nice, sharp edged rock. I threw it hard at Gannon. Got him in the leg. "Damn!" he roared out. He started for me but the man on the farmhouse porch began clanging his emergency bell.

"We better git, boss," Gannon's assistant said.

I stood at the closed gate to shove down the latch. Gannon came up to me. "I'll get you, girl, as well as I'll get that nigger I came for." He leaned down to look me squarely in the face. "Something about you, girl, mark me, I won't be forgetting you." With that he turned his horse and the two of them galloped away.

I ran to the house. The farmer and now his wife, helped Mr. Peterson out of the buggy and up the steps. I took hold of the horse's bridle. Mr. Peterson had been shot in the hand. He bled quite a bit.

"We'll send Amos for the doctor," the farmer's wife said.

"No need," Mr. Peterson said.

"Stop your protesting, Seth," the farmer said. A boy somewhat older than me came out of the house. "Amos, ride over to Doctor Berkel and bring him back."

The boy Amos nodded, and then ran towards the barn to get a horse.

"And who is this?" the wife asked about me.

"Miss Evans."

"Miss Evans, you are safe now. Come in."

"These are the Olmsted's, Miss Laura."

"Hello, how do you do?"

"You poor child," Mrs Olmsted said. They helped Mr. Peterson to a chair in the front room. Mrs. Olmsted then went to retrieve water and rags to clean Mr. Peterson's wound while they waited for the doctor.

"She's from Trenton," Mr. Peterson explained to Mr. Olmsted. "May she stay with you until we can reunite her with her family?"

"Certainly."

Mrs. Olmsted returned. She set about cleaning Mr. Peterson's wound. A young woman entered the room. "Sarah, show Miss Evans where she can wash up," Mrs. Olmsted said. "This is our daughter, Miss Evans. Go with her."

I followed instructions. Sarah led me to a small room next to the kitchen. Inside was a basin and soap for washing up. I wished for a shower, with tons of hot water running over me. But instead, all I could do was wash my face and hands, which were both considerably dirty. Sarah left me for privacy. I removed my hat, splashed water on my face, soaped it, and scrubbed it clean. I knew my hair must be a mess. I looked around for a brush. I found a comb. It would be painful but I had to comb my hair. I removed the ribbon which held it back. It fell down around my shoulders. That is when I knew my troubles were more serious than knowing the location of the time chair. Because instead of my reddish brown tresses, my hair was now jet black. I stood still in my shock for several moments. I shook it, seeing if it was dirt that had turned it black. Only a bit of dust came out. I examined it closely. It was indeed black.

"This is what Lamentations was talking about." I sat on the stool near the table. I looked down at my clothes. They were full of dust. I curled my toes in my boots. The boots seemed small on me.

I looked around the room for a mirror. There one stood, on top of a cabinet. In apprehension I approached it. I nearly fainted when I saw the girl returning my gaze. I *was* a different person, not the Ell who had left Trenton the night before. This Ell was nearly the same body type, but her coloring was so different from my own. Not only was my hair black, my eyes were a deep brown. My lips were fuller, and my nose straighter. I drew closer. When I was eight, my nose had been broken by a fly ball I had missed catching during a baseball game. My nose was supposed to have a slight bend and a small hump where the break had been. There was no hump. Yet that was not the worst shocker. My skin was darker. Olive in tone.

"What have I done?" I whispered. "What has happened?" I then collapsed. Fainting was a mercy.

Chapter Four

Mrs. Olmsted

I awoke in a dark and silent room. The only sound I heard was my own breathing. The only thing my eyes saw was the blankness afforded by the predawn. After awhile, my eyes adjusted. I could make out a chair, a dresser and the curtains drawn across the back window. I threw off the blanket. The morning was still cool and I was dressed only in my underclothes. As I sat up, I could hear a clanking of metal coming from the outdoors. At the window, I carefully pulled back the curtain to peer out below. It was Sarah, making her way to the barn with a pair of milk pails in her one hand, and an apron clutched in the other. When she disappeared into the barn, I returned to bed. The fatigue of the last two days still weighted me down. I soon fell back to sleep.

I dreamed. It began with my pocket watch, its tiny red light slowly blinking on and off. From the periphery, I could see the chair appear. It wasn't a solid mass at all. More like a shimmering apparition. Nonetheless, I attempted to sit on it. I could see myself fall, as well as feel my body hit the ground. While I sat there, my mother's voice drifted across the scene. "Ell? Ell?"

My mouth moved as if to form words, but no sound would come out. I ran toward her voice, but the chain attached to the watch was attached to the chair on its other end. It jerked me back. The watch's light kept blinking, off then on, off then on.

From the other side, a dog barked. My mouth formed the name, "Plato," but as with my mother, no sound came of it. I struggled to walk towards the barking, again, the watch's chain kept me tied to the chair.

"Ell?" A man's voice said, one I didn't recognize. "Ell?" he repeated. Finally, I was able to say, "What?" The answer came back, "Ell, why didn't you lie?" I struggled to run into the darkness to see who spoke, and what dog barked? However I tried, the struggle of tugging against the chair was futile. A strong light eased over my face.

"How can I lie?" It was a whisper that echoed around, a sound that was swallowed by the brightness of the light.

My eyes opened to the brightness of the sun streaming through the upper windows above the bed. It fell across my face. I quickly stood up, found my clothes and then hurriedly dressed. The boots were left off as I did not want to make a sound walking through the house. I opened the door and then listened. Muffled voices traveled up from the downstairs. I poked my head out. No one was in the hallway or near the stairwell. I crept out on my tiptoes, made my way to the stairwell. The voices grew louder though no one could be seen in the hall. I lightly walked down the first flight of steps, pausing at the landing. From that vantage point the kitchen door could be seen. The voices emanated from that room. I went down a few more steps. The voices became clearer.

"She is a well nourished child," a man's voice said. "But peculiar in a way I cannot put my finger on, except to say I cannot tell you her age."

"Hmm, I must agree with you, Dr. Berkel. There is something different about her. When we removed her outer garments, her under garments were, well strange." I recognized the voice of Mrs. Olmsted.

"Strange? How?"

"Her camisole. Nothing, well, girlish about it. More like something a boy would wear," Mrs. Olmsted said.

"Perhaps her family is quite poor, Emily, and that is all they can afford." This was Mr. Olmsted speaking.

"As well formed as she is?" This was Dr. Berkel speaking again. "Or do they have particular beliefs about women?"

Just then a woman's skirt and shoes were seen walking near the kitchen door. I backed away to hide behind the landing wall.

"For the life of me I cannot understand how she got to Philadelphia, or how she became entangled with Gannon." This was Mr. Peterson speaking.

"He is a brute, makes all other slavers seem kind," Mr. Olmsted said.

"Whatever the truth is, *we* don't want to know it," Mrs. Olmsted said.

"Neither do I." Mr. Peterson said. "And now, I best be going. I leave her in your trustworthy hands."

"We will see to it, Seth," Mr. Olmsted said.

The chairs scraped the floor as they were pushed back from the table. I turned to run back up to the room, but Amos stood in my way.

"Don't worry, they will go out the back way." He whispered.

"Oh."

"Breakfast is waiting for you."

"Amos?"

"Yes?"

"Will you help me get back to Philadelphia?"

"I thought you are from Trenton?" Amos looked at me with furrowed brows.

"I am, but I can't go back there. Not just yet."

Amos started to say something but the voices returned to the kitchen.

"I don't like it, Thomas, I don't like it at all." It was Mrs. Olmsted speaking. "Sarah, you go wake her."

"Hold on there daughter." Mr. Olmsted spoke. "Other than her name, you are to know nothing of her. Is that understood?"

"Yes father."

Sarah came out of the kitchen. Amos grabbed my arm and led me back to the stairs. He opened the door to the room I had slept in. "I'll help you," he whispered as he shoved me in. He closed the door behind me. I quickly sat in the chair as if I had been waiting. Soon, there was a light knock on the door.

"Enter," I said.

Sarah walked in. "Oh, you're up. Well, good morning. There is breakfast waiting for you, in the kitchen."

"Thank you."

Sarah led me out of the room. In the kitchen, only Mrs. Olmsted remained. She smiled, indicated with her hand I should sit at the place set for me. "Eat all you want, child."

"Yes ma'am, thank you ma'am."

Mrs. Olmsted turned to washing the dishes. Sarah cleaned the work table. Both worked quickly and

44

efficiently. Using a system that had been practiced a hundred times, the women rendered everything around me clean with every dish except the ones I ate on, put in its proper place. I ate quickly as I did not want to impede their progress. My preadolescent age afforded me an appetite like an adult. I finished the sausage and gravy on my plate. I cut a slice of bread and then spread it generously with the fresh butter that was in front of me. Of all the foods I have tasted, nothing is as delicious as butter made at home. I had a second slice. Then a third, which I used to wipe my plate clean..

"Thank you, Mrs. Olmsted. It was delicious."

Mrs. Olmsted smiled at me. I took the plate to the wash sink and washed it myself.

"You're a good girl. Now let's comb that hair of yours, and then we'll talk of returning you to your family back in Trenton." Mrs. Olmsted took my arm and sat me down at the table. "Sarah? Where is that comb and hair pins?"

"Why is Amos taking out the buggy?" Sarah asked.

"Amos is driving her to the ferry."

Waiting for Sarah to get the hair things, I stood at the back window. watching Amos pull the buggy out from the its shed attached to the horse barn. He took a rag and wiped the seat off. He then turned his attention to the harness.

With brush in hand, Mrs. Olmsted worked on my new, black tresses that were quite long. I had never had long hair in my life, for the daily goings on of Ell Evans were of such intense activity that my hair was kept just long enough for a short ponytail. That auburn hair had been wavy and easy to curl. This new hair, was not only long it was straight. Mrs. Olmsted laid into it with a vengeance for it had become tangled due to the previous days activities. With such hair as I now had, there could be no real gentleness with it for it was thick, heavy, making it difficult to sort through. As she worked, I began to think. How had this happened? There was no doubt in my mind that I had done something foolish in 1924 Trenton. But what? I replayed that night's terror over and over again. I had no ideas as to what I had done.

My thoughts then turned to Plato. He had started this mess by running out into the street, and now? Now he was probably dead. Why had he jumped into the time chair in the first place? My thoughts were cut short by Mrs Olmsted. She had found a snarl so thick my head was pulled back in a jerk. I was already near tears over Plato but that only made me lose control. I burst into tears.

"I am so sorry, dear, so sorry." Mrs. Olmsted put her arm around my shoulder to comfort me.

"It's my dog," I sobbed.

"What about your dog?"

"He was shot last night."

"By Gannon?"

I nodded my head.

"I will instruct Amos to take you and to go look for him. Then we can bury him properly, and you can say your farewells."

"Tha-thank you," was all I could get out of my mouth.

By the time Mrs. Olmsted finished combing my new locks, Amos had harnessed up a bay colored horse to the buggy. Sarah walked to the back door and opened it. "Come in, Mother wants to talk to you," she called out to him. Amos brushed off his boots before stepping into his mother's tidy kitchen.

"Tell him about where you think the dog was when he was shot."

"What dog?" Amos asked.

"She had a dog with her."

"Gannon began shooting before we got to your gate. I heard him yelp, like he was hurt."

"Take her down about mile, check the west side of the road and then the east side as you come back."

"Yes Mother." Amos returned to the buggy outside.

"I think a nice braid down the back would be best with this hair. What do you think?"

I nodded in agreement. What else could I do with this unknown quality that was my head of hair but leave it to someone else to decide? Mrs. Olmsted pulled my hair back off my face and gathered it around to my neck. Pulling firmly, she began the process of twisting my unruly tresses into a controlled mass that fell nearly to my waist. She tied off the end of this braid with a lovely red ribbon. She took a second piece of ribbon, this one a lively pink, rolled it up, and placed it in my hand.

"In case the red becomes undone, you will have a spare."

"Thank you, Mrs. Olmsted. I will never forget your kindness."

Mrs. Olmsted patted my hand. "I understand you have been through an ordeal, and I cannot know the whys and wherefores of it. But when it comes to slavers and such, we keep our mouths shut, and forget things that people tell us. The less we know, the less we have to tell."

"I understand, Mrs. Olmsted."

"That doesn't stop me from praying for you. I will pray hard, dear, very hard for I think you are in more trouble than we can know. The Lord tells us to have no fear. Therefore, keep your chin firm, and up."

I broke into tears again, not so much for her words of kindness and advice, but for the acknowledgement she gave my plight.

Sarah brought me my hat. I smiled, weakly, as I took it from her. "Amos is waiting."

Mrs. Olmsted tied the hat onto my head. "Go now and look for your dog." She walked to the open door and spoke out to Amos. "Bring the dog back here. We will take care of it."

"Yes, mother."

Outside, I tucked the pink ribbon into the little purse tied to my waist, and then climbed into the buggy next to Amos. He clicked the horse forward. As we drove out of the yard, I turned to wave at the stern yet loving Mrs. Olmsted. I doubted I would ever see her again. I wanted to blow her a kiss with my hand, but thought that might be too modern. In my mind I did just that. I would always love her for these few hours of her understanding even though she knew nothing of me. Except that I was a human being in trouble. In my later years, as I think of Mrs. Olmsted, I understand how she felt that it was not her duty to help me, or others for that matter. It was her delight.

Chapter Five

Moses

We drove down the country lane in silence. No matter what Mrs. Olmsted had said about not being afraid, I was quite afraid. The cool, summer morning weather should have been calming. It was not. My eyes darted from side to side of the road, as my heart beat rapidly and my mind both wanted and did not want to know what had happened to Plato. Amos too kept his eyes peeled for the body of a dark red and white Springer Spaniel. Though I barely knew the dog, for some reason I felt he was mine and had been mine for a much longer time than the past two days.

Or was it more than two days that I had known him? A new, more powerful, unsettling feeling entered my being. Not only I had lost my self, I had lost track of time. I vowed that I would not, if I could back to Trenton 1974, that I would not ever time travel again.

The buggy halted.

"What's that?" Amos whispered.

Something moved just beyond the row of trees that lined the field. It was low to the ground, moving slowly. My heart beat faster. "Plato?" I whispered.

I jumped down and ran towards him. I was afraid, and relieved. Drawing closer to him, I could see he was injured. I couldn't see where exactly. But the life was in him as he crawled along on his belly. "Plato!"

He stopped, turned his head toward me. His tail wagged. He gave a sort of low moan. I knelt down beside him. "It's alright, fella, I'm here. I'll see to it." I petted his head gently. He licked my hand.

Amos was close behind. "Let's turn him over and see what the problem is."

Together we gently rolled his body to his side so that we could see where he was hurt. It was his back left leg.

"There's where the bullet hit," Amos said pointing to a wound that had stopped bleeding. "He licked the wound clean. Yes, I think he'll be fine." Amos pressed gently down on the leg. Plato moaned. "Leg might be broke. Probably from the impact. We can take him to Doc's house."

"The local veterinarian?"

"No, we don't have one hereabouts. Doctor Berkel, who fixed up Mr. Paterson." Amos gently picked up Plato in his arms. "Doc will treat Plato."

I followed Amos back to the buggy. He gently placed him in the back in the luggage rack.

"Doc's not too far away. Good thing because we need to go slow so not to jar him none."

"Thank you."

We rode along in silence. The slow clip-clop of the horse's hooves mixed with the quiet of the country morning lured me into a meditative thinking. I needed to find a way to fix my predicament. As much as I wanted to return to the Trenton of 1974, I had to get back to the city of 1924. That is where the thing, whatever it was that had happened, that is where the change to my person had happened. That is where I had to go to fix it.

Plato too concerned me. Something about him, and there again I couldn't tell what, but Plato had a mind of his own, a will that was forceful. It was almost as if he purposely caused things to happen.

My thoughts turned to the Old Man. Would he find me? Did he know that I was gone in time? Or did he think I had gone back home? Now a restlessness invaded me. The chair is the only thing that could help me. I had to get back to it. Though things looked different in the daylight, I was confident I could, with Plato's help, find it.

I glanced at Amos. I felt I could trust him. But how to approach him? Make him a friend.

"Amos?"

"Yes miss?"

"My name is Ell."

"I'm not supposed to know that, miss." Amos' voice made that slight skip that adolescent boys make when speaking.

"Please, stop calling me miss."

"Why?"

"Because I am a battle weary girl of nearly twelve, and I have to fix…my mistakes."

"I don't understand you."

"No, you can't, of course. If I were to tell you *everything*, you would think me mad."

"Once the dog is attended to, I'll take you to the ferry. I can cross with you, take you all the way home. That is what my father would want me to do."

"What if you disobey him?"

"Miss?"

"Ell, the name is Ell."

"Ell. Why would you want me to disobey my father?"

"Because it is a part of growing up. Of being independent. Of doing something on your own."

"What are you talking about?" Amos turned the buggy onto a small lane. A wooden sign said, "Elias Berkel, M.D." At the end of the lane was a neat and tidy white, clapboard house.

"I need you to take us to a place near the river."

"Is that all?" Amos smiled broadly. "I can do that before I take you to the ferry."

"But I don't want to go to the ferry." I looked at Amos who was scrutinizing me. "It's like this. I have an item that I must retrieve."

"Oh, you left something?"

I nodded my head vigorously.

"I don't see why, after we get that item, you don't want to go to the ferry?"

An answer to that question would take some thinking. It was time to tell one of those time traveler lies. On second thought, the chair was not that far from Philadelphia. Plato and I could disappear into the woods. No. That wouldn't work. Amos was too smart, too competent to allow me to disappear. He would look for me. Besides, Plato wouldn't be able to move very fast. Fact was, I needed Amos to cooperate with me.

"About taking me to the river."

"Yes?"

"You can help me get the thing I need to get, and then can you take me to Philadelphia?"

We drove along in silence for a moment.

"You know what I think? I think you don't want to go home." Amos pulled up on the reins in front of Dr. Berkel's house. "Let's take the dog in."

Amos jumped down, came around first to help me down, and then he went into the back to pickup Plato.

A side door to the house opened. Dr. Berkel came out. "What's that you got there, Amos?"

"This is Plato, her dog." Amos nodded his chin toward me.

Dr. Berkel looked over the dog. "Was your dog shot last night by Gannon?"

I nodded my head and then burst into tears. Dr. Berkel looked at me with sympathy. "Bring the dog inside."

The three of us went into Dr. Berkel's examination room. Amos placed him on the examination table. Dr. Berkel bent over Plato to probe the wound. Plato groaned. He inspected the leg. Plato was patient, but in pain. He put his head into my hands.

"Leg is not broke, but see here?" Dr. Berkel pointed to a wound we hadn't noticed before on the other side of Plato's leg. "That is what's called an exit wound. Bullet went straight through him." Dr. Berkel cleaned the wound. Plato was patient. He knew we were helping him. He then smeared salve on the entrance and exit points. After that, he bandaged the leg.

"You, young lady, and your dog are lucky." Dr Berkel now filled a small jar with the salve. "That Gannon is a careless man. One of these days he's going to kill someone." Dr. Berkel handed the jar of salve to me. "Use this on both sides of the wound, two times a day." He then handed me a small roll of bandages. "Change the bandage every morning for a week. He should be just fine, though you need to keep him off that leg as much as possible."

"Yes Dr. Berkel. Thank you Dr. Berkel."

"Have your parents send me two dollars when you get home."

"Yes, Dr. Berkel.

Amos carried Plato out to the buggy.

"Are you going home?" He looked me steadily in the eyes.

"Eventually."

"Eventually?" Dr. Berkel looked at me the way a thinking man does when he is weighing options. He was every bit the scientist. He then took a piece of paper and wrote down his address.

"Eventually remember to send me those two dollars," he said as he handed me the paper.

"I will." I stuffed the paper into my purse.

When I got out to the buggy, Amos had placed Plato on the floor.

"About that item," I said.

"The one by the river?" Amos clucked the horse forward. He gave me a side glance. "You are trouble."

Amos turned the buggy towards the road. For a mile or so we kept silent. Plato fell asleep. The fields of wheat and corn gave way to a large pasture filled with cows on one side, and a vegetable farm on the other. The cow pasture ended where the small forest began. Ahead of us the buildings of Philadelphia filled up the horizon like a miniature city. To the left, the road Lamentation's and I had taken into the city the night before went off on an angle toward the forest.

"Over there." I pointed with my chin.

"That's the new city road. It ends just shy of the trees."

"Right. It's beyond the road."

"What is?"

"To tell you, I have to swear you to secrecy."

"If you are talking about rescuing runaways, well, we are used to secrecy."

"This is something else."

Amos turned to me.

"What I mean to say…it's something different." I gave him a slight smile. "Will you swear to secrecy?"

"I can't swear. Quakers don't take oaths. Therefore, I will give you my promise. Your secret is safe with me."

We came to a small road, a broad path really, that connected to the city road at an angle. Amos took this road. It was rutted and slightly muddy between the ruts. The buggy felt like a ship at sea it swayed so. Plato had to be held down so that he wouldn't slip out. He wagged his tail. He knew we didn't discomfort him on purpose. After a few minutes of this we came to the new road. The smoother ride was a relief. It too, however, ended. Beyond it was more uneven ground.

"River's right there." Amos pointed to his right. "Is this the place you wanted? Because there looks to be something strange looking in the trees there."

He pulled the horse to a stop and then jumped out of the buggy. I followed him. There it was. The chair sitting in between two large pines. But that is not where I have left it. I approached it with caution.

"What is that?"

"You can't know, except that it is a machine that I need ever so much. So very much."

"Looks like a chair to me. What sort of machine is a chair?" He looked up at the glass. "Why the windows?"

"Amos, please, don't ask." I reached into my little purse for the watch. I opened it. To my amazement, the little light blinked on and off! "Oh!" In gratitude, I clutched the watch to my chest.

"What is it?"

"It's working!" I took hold of Amos' shoulders, squeezing them hard. "It's a miracle! Oh thank you, Amos, thank you!" Tears of relief came down my cheek. I walked around to peek at the dials. They blinked. The destination dial read 1854. The return dial read 1974. I nearly fainted in the anticipation of rectifying my problem. On the ground I noticed that there was another set of drag marks. Had someone else found the chair and moved it? I checked the chair itself. All seemed normal. I sat. I changed the destination dial to read 1974. Next, I adjusted the return dial to 1854.

"Amos?"

"Yes?"

"We need to put Plato into the chair."

Amos did as I asked, gently placing Plato on the seat of the chair.

"Now, I am making the machine work. You need to stand off aways."

"Is it dangerous?"

"If you stand too close, yes."

Amos walked off about fifteen feet. I flicked the switch and waited. Nothing happened. I repeated the action. Still nothing.

"What is the matter, Ell?"

"I don't know." I got out of the chair to walk around to the back. I lifted up the cover to the clock box. The clock was gone. I gasped.

Amos walked back to me. "Something's missing, huh?"

"It's not so much a something, as a somebody who took something."

"You are the strangest girl." Amos sat on the chair and petted Plato.

I took a turn around the area, looking for clues as to who had used the chair. The Old Man was my first thought. That he had come looking for me, and I was no where near the chair to be found. Now I wished I had stayed by the chair last night. As for the present moment, there was nothing to do, except go back into the city. That, my gut told me, is where the Old Man looked for me.

"Come on. We have to find someone in Philadelphia."

It did not take us long to find ourselves in the middle of Colored Town. I recognized Mrs. Bishop's shop right away. I ran in hoping to find Lamentations there, though why he should be there I didn't know. My determination had taken over, and all that I could see in front of me was the success of my new mission: to find the Old Man or have him find me.

Mrs. Bishop recognized me right away. She tended to her customers, and when they had left, she turned to me.

"Why, what are you doing here, miss?"

"Please, Mrs. Bishop, I have a huge favor to ask of you."

"Does this have to do with your friend?"

I nodded.

"And where is Mr. Peterson?" Mrs. Bishop looked out the window. "Where is he?"

"Gannon followed us. He shot Mr. Peterson in the hand." I told her of the ordeal, without mentioning the Olmsted's by name. I had learned quickly about the necessity for keeping information to myself. So details, especially names, were left out.

"Child, how did you come to find yourself wrapped up in this business?"

"Isn't it best that you don't know?"

Mrs. Bishop sighed deeply. "Yes, of course. But you need your friend. Why?"

"Only he can help me out of this difficulty."

Mrs. Bishop studied me with a keen eye. She took a deep breath.

"Someone came in here this morning asking about a young girl about your age. But the description didn't quite fit. That's why I kept my tongue. But I think it was you he was after."

"Who?"

Mrs. Bishop kept her tongue again.

"Just tell me what he looked like?"

"An older gentleman. Of color."

"The Old Man, oh, the Old Man."

"Tell me no names."

"I won't. But if he should come back, tell him…" I had to think of some code that the Old Man would know. Then it came to me. "If he should come back, tell him the girl has a wounded dog."

"If he should come back?"

I took Mrs. Bishops' hand in mine. "He is sort of a guardian angel. Please, now, my friend?"

"Timothy!"

A young black man poked his head through the curtained doorway.

"I have to go out. Mind the shop."

Timothy nodded his head as he came out of the storeroom and we went in. Mrs. Bishop removed her apron, put on her hat, and then grabbed her parasol. We then went out the back door into the same alleyway Mr. Peterson and I had escaped down the night before. It looked different in the daylight. Mrs. Bishop then led me to the street. Amos sat in the buggy, watching the many people that made their way along the sidewalks and street. Plato kept his chin on his two front paws, minding his own business.

"I have a buggy," I said pointing to Amos.

"He best stay put. Go tell him, and then meet me across the street."

I obeyed Mrs. Bishop. Amos pulled his hat down over his eyes and leaned back. He would snooze. Mrs. Bishop led me up the alley. That alley led to another that crossed it. We turned east. This alley was narrower and could tolerate only foot traffic. After we passed several buildings, we came to one that had a sign hanging out that said, "Mrs. Tatum's Boarding House." We walked into a small foyer. There, an older man stood behind a counter. Mrs. Bishop did not say a thing to this man. She took instead a sheet of paper from the counter, and with the pencil that sat next to it, she wrote a note. This note she folded neatly into thirds. This she handed to the man. He was about to ring the bell on the countertop, but Mrs. Bishop stopped him.

"To be delivered, *personally*."

The man nodded that he understood. He walked out from around the counter, took the note from Mrs. Bishop's hand, and then headed up the stairs. We sat down on a bench to wait. While we did, the front door opened and several men entered. One rang the bell.

"He'll be back presently," Mrs. Bishop said to the men.

A young boy came out to the counter.

"Yes sirs?" he said to the men.

"We would like rooms."

"We are filled up until Thursday. You can try Mrs. Sunders or the camp."

"We just came from the camp," one of the men said.

"Mrs. Sunders is three blocks west of here."

The men briefly spoke among themselves and then tipping their hats to Mrs. Bishop and myself, they left. The boy looked at me with curiosity. It was rare to see a white girl in this establishment.

The man came down the stairs. "You can go up, Mrs. Bishop. But the girl got to stay here."

Mrs. Bishop stood. "I'll send for you," she said to me before following the man up the stairs.

I waited. After a few moments, the man came back down the stairs. He returned to his work back behind the counter. I looked up at the clock. It said 12:13. I popped open my stop watch. The red light wasn't blinking. It was too far away to get a reading from the machine. The time was correct. Odd, I thought. How did my watch know the local time?

After minutes passed, I grew tired of sitting. I stood and paced a bit.

"Why don't you amuse yourself in the parlor," the man said to me. He came around and opened the door to a small room filled with stuffed chairs and a piano.

"May I? I said pointing to the piano. I then stopped myself. I didn't know how to play the piano. Yet I did.

"You may play, miss." The man opened the cover to expose the keyboard. He then adjusted the seat to fit my height, after which he left the room to resume his duties.

The piano was a large upright made of oak with ornately carved legs. The straight sides of the music stand were carved to represent vines that twisted around. At the top, the ends of the vines on either side ended in large leaves that worked as an extension of the stand. This made it possible for the player to place a broad sheet of music on it. I touched a key. Slightly out-of-tune, my mind said. I jerked my hand back. How did I know that? I was not musical. Yet here I was with a desire to play an instrument I had never played but somehow knew how to play. I sat on the stool. I placed my hands on the keys. Instinctively, they moved, and I played something. What is this? Yes, it is Beethoven's *Moonlight Sonata*. I jumped up from the stool. How did I know this?!

"Oh, don't stop miss. That was lovely. Keep playing," the man at the counter called out.

I returned to the stool, brushed my fear aside and continued to play the sonata where I had left off. Somehow the music I didn't know soothed me. Or the act of playing it did. It was my heart that knew the piece, my ears and emotions knew it, and my hands followed. This was all a part of the new me, the one I was beginning to recognize. I focused on the playing and didn't hear the steps that came down the stairs and into the room. It was when the shadow fell across the keyboard that I perceived the presence of others in the room with me. I stopped. My eyes went to the body that created the shadow. And there, leaning against the door frame of the room, listening, was Lamentations.

I ran to him, threw my arms around him and burst into tears. He was surprised, but kind. He allowed me a few seconds before taking my arms away.

"We can't be doing that here, miss," he said softly.

"I'm, I'm happy to see you, Mr. Lamentations, and relieved that you haven't left yet."

"This is her?" a deep woman's voice said.

I turned to look to see who spoke. It was a small black woman, sturdy, with chestnut colored skin and dark eyes that saw everything. Across her left forehead, and down to the temple there was a pronounced scar. She stood perfectly still while she observed the emotional scene before her. Her eyes rested on me.

"Yes, Mrs. Tubman, this is the young lady."

"You found Moses?" I said.

"Moses found me."

Mrs. Tubman laughed, a hardy, throat laugh. Lamentations smiled broadly. He then became serious.

"You'll help me, then?" He asked me.

Mrs. Tubman too, looked serious.

"Close the door," she said to Lamentations. She took my hand, led me to one of the chairs, and pointed to it. I sat. She sat opposite. "Lamentations tells me you are a strange child, a girl from another country. I asked him if you were Canadian. He said no, further away."

"I didn't say, Miss Ell, I didn't say for sure," Lamentations assured me.

"And I didn't ask any further, except I wanted to know if we could rely on you to help us find his sister?"

"How would I do that?"

"We have a plan."

"And that plan is?" Inside, my nerves tingled in anticipation.

"That you travel to Baltimore as a young lady of wealth."

"And in Baltimore, how would I find his sister?"

"We have *friends* that would help you manage this. As a young lady of position, you would be befriended by the right sorts of people. And they would get you close to the Warton family. Lavinia Warton owns the sister." Mrs.

Tubman reached down to run her fingers across the fabric of my skirt. "You would have to look the part."

"And how do I do that?"

Mrs. Tubman looked back to Lamentations. "Fetch Mrs. Bishop."

When Mrs. Bishop entered, Mrs. Tubman motioned for her to come near. "Feel that fabric. Quality or not?"

Mrs. Bishop now ran her fingers against the fabric of my skirt. "Thin. Not good enough for what we spoke of."

"Can you fix it?"

"I know those who can."

"Wait for us."

Mrs. Bishop left the room. Mrs. Tubman waited until the door was shut. She then leaned forward to speak to me a low tones.

"You will need clothing worthy of the position. Those Southern women know their quality as they hate an intruder who does not meet their expectations. They are ladies of privilege. And of despair. As you will find out."

"Where do I find the clothing that meets their expectations?"

"Mrs. Bishop will take care of that." Mrs. Tubman's face betrayed no emotions, only business.

We sat in silence for a moment, each one thinking our own thoughts.

"Mrs. Tubman, you must have confidence that I can do this thing."

"As Lamentations has said, you belong somewhere else. This makes you hard to place." She brought her hand up to her face, stroked her cheeks, fingers on one side, thumb on the other. "I say you come from another country." She fell silent.

I looked over to Lamentations. He was pleading with his eyes. In my mind, I assessed my situation. I knew the Old Man was in town. How, I wondered, could the Old Man find me if I traveled down to Baltimore? And what of Lamentations? He was now in his timeline, so my duty, my rational side told me, was over. I had brought him back. It's not up to me to do anything further. My real purpose should be to return to my rightful place in time. In that way, I would cause no further problems, for to help Lamentations with his sister meant changing history.

Or did it? How did I know what had happened with Lamentations and his sister? That brought in a second thought. Did I need Lamentations to return with me to 1924 to change the situation caused by Plato? Would Lamentations consider returning with me? He now had met Mrs. Tubman, the Moses he needed so that his sister could be rescued and led to freedom. Why would he return to Trenton 1924 with me? That could only mean more trouble for him.

There was more to the equation than Lamentations and his needs. There was that other, new side of me, the one who played Beethoven from memory. What had happened to change me, and what did I need to change to rectify that? I took a deep breath. The original side of me now took over. That is the real Ell, the girl looking for authentic knowledge by way of adventure. That Ell was, and is, on a journey, to learn specific things no matter where they take her. True, she is not to make changes in history's events, but why not help folks help themselves?

The Old Man's rules were difficult to stick to, but the opportunity to learn something first hand intrigued me beyond my ability to resist.

"There are," I began, looking steadily at Mrs. Tubman, "certain rules I must obey. Please don't ask where these rules come from."

"I understand, and I won't ask."

I glanced over at the piano. If I was to be a rich girl, that new skill would come in handy. I got up and went to the keyboard, tinkled a few keys. "I shall be, " I paused and remembered something my mother had told me about my ability to mimic an English accent. I cleared my throat, and with my most dignified voice, and using the English accent I had heard on so many shows from Britain, I then said, "I shall be Miss Ellen Bennet, a cousin, from England."

Mrs. Tubman turned her head and looked at me sideways. "That sounds real to me."

"I watch- I mean I have been to many plays with English actors. I can imitate well, or so my mother says."

"I hope your mother is correct."

"She is." I closed my eyes to picture my mother telling me I sounded like Vanessa Redgrave.

"Who," I opened my eyes, "is this Warton family?"

It was the question that sealed my fate. Or rather, it sealed our fate, for now we were a group effort.

Chapter 6

Baltimore

Mrs. Bishop turned her friends loose on me. I was taken to a dress shop on Baker Street where a Mrs. Cowell instructed her girls to disrobe me and then measure me, head to foot. They sent for a shoe maker, a corset maker, and a hat maker. One woman made camisoles and slips for me, which they referred to as shifts. Another occupied her time by sewing stockings. A third lady made blouses. Mrs. Cowell was a master tailor. It was she who designed and cut my several outfits. These she handed off to a series of seamstresses who quickly set about to sewing up the garments. There was not a sewing machine anywhere. These women and girls sewed each seam by hand.

Mrs. Cowell, before any dress or skirt or jacket was finished, made certain that the fit was impeccable. By the end of the first day, one dress was finished. In a week, a trunk was filled with dresses, two skirts with matching jackets, blouses, petticoats, shifts, camisoles, stockings and shoes. A hat box held three hats and many ribbons for my hair.

Plato grew strong. He was fussed over by the ladies as he rested in their various shops. Their children took him for walks, helping him as he limped along. Plato was shown tenderness, as was I. By the end of the week, he could walk well enough, though his slight limp was still with him. On the day before I was to leave, Plato was given a finely made leather collar with a matching lead. This was Mr. Cowell's work. Mrs. Cowell then gave me a dress made of lace that took everyone's breath away.

"For church on Sundays," Mrs. Cowell said. "Or elegant dinner parties."

"The Wartons go to church," Lamentations concurred. "And Mr. Warton likes to have folks over. He a proud man."

"What church?" I asked.

"You will find out," Mrs. Tubman told me in a matter-of-fact way.

"She will need a servant," Mrs. Bishop said.

"Who would risk it?" Mrs. Cowell asked.

"Never mind that. It's been arranged," Mrs. Tubman said. She then turned to me. "You must obey me in all things." I nodded. She turned to Lamentations. "You as well. When I tell you to take on silence, take it on. If I say run, you run."

"Yes ma'am."

"You're taken' on a terrible risk. But we will find your sister, and get her away, as long as she is willin'."

"She might not be?" I asked.

"That is so. The way up to freedom is long and hard. We battle bugs and snakes and dogs and bad men. You know about the bad men. Though many may wish it, to have their freedom, not everyone is willin' to die tryin' for it."

"I can't believe that," I said.

"Don't argue with Mrs. Tubman, child. She know what she's saying," Mrs. Bishop said.

Mrs. Bishop was right to admonish. For what did I know of freedom, me a child of the twentieth century? It was a quality I took for granted. What I had seen with my own eyes was how *some* would risk everything for their liberty, including their very life. But not all Americans had fought in the American Revolution, not all Americans had desired their independence from Britain. Why should I think one girl, not much older than I was, why should she risk all for a highly risky flight from the life she knew? I took on the silence.

The next day, I wore one of my new outfits, the one Mrs. Cowell called a traveling suit. It was a soft brown, with a ruffle along the bottom of the skirt, and matching ruffles that ran the length of the sleeves. Underneath the skirt I wore a rather stiff petticoat that flared out my skirt. The blouse was a creamy white. It was, to my estimation, one of Mrs. Cowell's masterpieces.

I was a bit apprehensive about traveling on my own, aside from Mrs. Tubman's assurances that I would have a companion. Who this companion was no one would tell me. In their world, secrets were the way of doing things as the less we know about the others the better it will be. A stranger had dropped me, Plato and my luggage off at the train station. All he did after I stood on the platform was to press a ticket into my hands. He did not even say good bye. Working within the underground railroad was like time travel; lies and secrets and keeping one's mouth shut was the only true security we had.

My biggest concerns were Gannon and his sidekick, the young man, who I learned was named Vigilis. What if they should take the train? Could the wounded Plato protect me? He seemed strong, though he still limped. I patted his head. He wagged his tail, vigorously. He stood close to me. He was my one assurance at that moment until I heard a familiar voice behind me.

"Lady Bennet?"

It was Martin. He was well dressed in a black suit, with the whitest shirt and a dark tie circling around a starched collar.

"Martin?"

He leaned down to whisper it near my ear. "Botlieb is the name."

"What are you doing here?" I whispered. I then turned my head to look around. Plato kept his tail going forcing his nose into Martin's hand.

"Don't look at anything but me." He motioned for a man to take my trunk and hatbox. "Take Lady Bennet's things to her private coach."

"Private coach?" I asked.

"Shssh. Now give me the dog's lead."

The man Martin had spoken to placed my luggage on a cart. Martin pointed out to him a small, private coach hooked up to the rear of the train. "I see it sir. Best be boarding sir as the train will leave in 10 minutes." The man headed toward the coach.

Martin petted Plato. He leaned down to his face. "Behave, eh?" He then turned to me, whispering, "You behave as well, ja?" He then said loudly, "Lady Bennet, shall we go?"

I turned to follow the luggage cart.

"Lady Ellen Bennet?" It was a woman's voice. "Ellen, there you are dear."

The woman speaking to me smiled gently without showing her teeth. She wore a traveling suit of gray, with a plain black hat veiled in grey. It was tied on with a ribbon that matched her suit. In her hand she held a hat box of dark brown. Next to her was a black boy a bit younger than me who pulled a small cart with two pieces of luggage on it.

I did not know this woman. Yet she knew me.

"Shall we board?" she said to me.

"We are boarding just now." I pointed to the private coach.

She turned to see the coach, turned back to me, with that same smile. I could see she was surprised but she wiped that surprise off her face. She was practiced in the art of flexibility for the sake of concealment. She smiled at me more broadly. She turned to Martin, held out her hand to him. "I am Miss Cameron, Lady Ellen's new American governess. I take it her parents told you of me?"

"Yes, they have," Martin said taking her hand. "I am, of course, her butler, Botlieb."

The woman looked askance at Martin. She didn't let on that anything perturbed her. She followed us to the coach, the black child pulling the cart with her luggage behind him.

I climbed the steps of the private coach to enter a world I did not know existed. The first room was elegantly appointed in lace curtains, two stuffed chairs by a window, a settee in the middle, and, on the other side, a table and two smaller, stuffed chairs under the window. Behind the settee was a curtain. I peeked behind it as Miss Cameron entered followed by Martin. Behind the curtain was a small galley kitchen. Beyond that, to the side, was a door. This door opened into a small bedroom, with two beds. Heavy velvet curtains covered the windows. To the other side stood a folding screen of pale yellow silk. All was luxurious. I wondered how Martin obtained such a train car. Martin, I began to learn, was resourceful.

"It's all very lovely, isn't it?" Miss Cameron said, placing her hatbox on the dresser near the door. She looked me fully in the eyes, making me a bit uncomfortable. She seemed to want to say something. She held her tongue.

"Botlieb is resourceful," I said in my best English accent, as a way of reassuring her that all was well, that Martin could be trusted.

"Come, let's settle in. We will not arrive in Baltimore til the morning."

Miss Cameron untied my hat, and then tidied my hair. "We will stay at the Lord Baltimore Hotel. We have a suite on the third floor. Of course I hadn't planned on the gentleman."

"I wouldn't concern myself, Miss Cameron, with Botlieb. He will manage."

"Yes." Miss Cameron unbuttoned my jacket. "It's a lovely blouse." She then leaned down to whisper into my ear. "You fit the role perfectly." With that she straightened her spine and walked out of the bedroom.

I gazed into the full length mirror in the corner. It was difficult to recognize myself. My hairstyle done up in my black tresses, my dark eyes, did make me look more elegant. The nose, mouth and shape of my lower face were the old Ell's. I paraded in front of the mirror, acting the part of the English aristocrat.

"Not too snobbish, eh?" Martin said as he brought the luggage into the room. "You must be at ease with your station in life."

"At ease?"

"Yes. As if you have always had everything including servants." He took hold of my chin and looked over my face. "You are at least one inch taller. Did you know that?"

"What's happened to me?"

"Something was changed, and now you are changed because of it. Something to do with your parents, or perhaps your grandparents. Have you been in Philadelphia this entire time?"

"No." I then told him about Trenton in 1924. His face took on a serious look. It frightened me.

"The professor went to look for you, in 1974. He could not find your parents."

Martin saw the startled look on my face.

"Not to worry. We will find the solution to this problem." He put his arm around my shoulders to reassure me. "Before we get to Baltimore I shall contact the Professor. For now, we must accomplish your purpose."

"Tea is served," Miss Cameron called out from the other room.

Tea? I had forgotten about the English and their tea. I hated tea, but there was nothing I could do about that. The hated stuff would have to be tolerated, whether I liked it or not. Fortunately Miss Cameron also had an ample supply of little cakes. Enough for us all, and Plato, who sat at attention near the table. He glanced at each of us, with hope in his eyes. Perhaps tea would not be so dreary after all. As we sat at table, the conversation turned to my pretend family, who they were, where they lived. I had already memorized all my relatives' names, so all that was left for me to do was to determine who I liked among my aunts, uncles and cousins. We had, in Philadelphia, decided that my parents should be dead, and I was being raised by an aunt, whose daughter lives in Philadelphia.

This story had been rehearsed throughout my visits with the dressmaker and the shoemaker and the hat maker. All that was left to me now was to convince George Warton that I was the genuine article so that he would introduce me to his daughter, who, we had been told, was to be Marini's new mistress.

"Your one goal is to wrest an invitation to Miss Lavinia's wedding," Miss Cameron said.

"She is marrying?"

"That is our latest information."

"Where does your information come from?" Martin asked.

"I am sorry, Botlieb, but that is not for you to know." Miss Cameron poured him more tea.

"I understand."

Martin seemed to like the tea. He drank it down without milk or sugar.

"How did a German gentlemen get to be an English butler?" Miss Cameron asked.

Martin smiled broadly. "I am sorry, Miss Cameron, but that is not for you to know."

"Touche, Mr. Botlieb, touche."

The train jerked into motion.

"We're off," Miss Cameron said.

Martin removed his pocket watch. I glanced over at it. It was much more masculine than mine, and a bit larger. He flicked it open. There, just as mine, was the small, pin sized red light. His was blinking, slowly. The chair could not be too far away. Secretly, I took mine out. My red light shone, but did not blink. I wondered why.

74

"It is 5 pm. We leave on time." He closed it and tucked it back into his vest pocket. "We stop in Wilmington to dine."

"I've plenty of sandwiches in my basket."

"Nein, Miss Cameron. We shall *dine* in Wilmington."

Miss Cameron leaned back in her chair. She smiled at Martin in that way I've seen women smile at men they like. Why shouldn't she like him? He was attractive and smart and one of the world's greatest adventurers. She didn't know that of him, that he was an outstanding man of all times. Yet she sensed that he had a significant capacity to take on danger with aplomb. All which made Martin intensely male. Of course I could only sense these things about him for I was too young and inexperienced in life to understand it fully. Later, as I grew up, then I would realize the importance of Martin, and how the success of our enterprise depended upon him. For Martin was a true gentleman, and as all men of such conduct are, he protected us.

After our tea, I was drilled again. Not only in my narrative, but in the way I walked, sat, shook hands, did a curtsey and spoke to my betters, peers and underlings. Here I was a twentieth century girl attempting to pass myself off as not only a nineteenth century girl, but as one whose station in life was quite restricted. I was not to be allowed any relaxation for fear that I would forget myself at a crucial moment. The two of them rehearsed me until we reached Wilmington. By then I felt I *was* Lady Ellen Bennet, daughter of the Viscount Perth, Lord Clive Bennet, deceased.

"I am starved," I said as we gathered our hats and gloves.

Baltimore

When we reached the train station platform, we were guided to a restaurant nearby. Martin thanked the man, but had him call a carriage instead. We were driven to a different restaurant, smaller, and more elegant. The owners greeted Martin with affection, sat us at a table, and then immediately brought out food for us. We ate steak and crabs, seasonal vegetables and topped it off with a wonderful cake. All this was accompanied by wines, which I was allowed to drink, though diluted. At the end of the meal, we were given small baskets of chocolates for our journey. And a steak for Plato. We returned to the train just in time, for the conductor looked for us. We boarded our coach, and no sooner had we closed the door than the train lurched forward nearly knocking us off our feet.

I was allowed to stay up, for an hour more, to read a book titled, *Pride and Prejudice* by Jane Austen. Sleep, however, claimed me long before that hour was up.

When I awoke, the train was still. In the other bed, Miss Cameron slept. I leaned over to lift the shade of the window near my bed. It was dawn. A low fog hugged the ground. The sound of voices drifted to me. I leaned my head against the window to get a fuller view. No one was in sight. Silently, I swung my legs down to the floor. I tiptoed around Miss Cameron's bed. The voices grew louder. I looked out the east side window. There, partially hidden by the shadows of pine trees, stood Martin and the Old Man. They were in deep conversation, a talk that went from arguing to exasperation from both. I stepped back from the window. I must have done something terribly wrong for them to argue like that. Still, I couldn't allow myself to think about it. There was too much riding on my shoulders for me to become saddened by my own failures. I would just have to carry on. Others depended on me.

Nothing matures us more like others depending on us.

Minutes later Martin returned. "You saw us?" he asked. I nodded. "Ell, Ellen, you must not worry. Everything will turn out well."

"You were arguing."

"We disagree about what must be done."

"What do *you* think must be done?"

"We continue as planned. When this Lamentations and his sister are safe, then we ask Lamentations to go back. And then everything must be repeated."

"What about Plato?"

"That is the slight problem."

"And the professor, what does he think should be done to make things right?"

"We go back now. To the warehouse. There we wait for Lamentations to come through, and then immediately send him back."

I sat on the settee, drawing my knees to my chin.

"Would that bring back my parents, and make me look the way I did?"

"Both ways it is possible for your parents to return." Martin sat down beside me. "What is important to you, Ell? Because even when we go back, there are no guarantees we fix all."

"I've made such a mess!"

"What is all this talk about?"

We had not seen Miss Cameron enter the front room.

"It is our business, Miss Cameron."

"Hmm." Miss Cameron tied her robe. "Let's have tea, shall we. By the time we dress, we will be in Baltimore." She slipped into the kitchen. "Lady Ellen," she called out, "do put on your robe. It's unseemly for a young lady to parade about her in nightdress."

After our morning tea, Miss Cameron helped me dress. She made it plain to me that she would see to my dressing from this point forward. I did as she said. She did my hair in braids that twisted across and stayed placed against the back of my head. She sent me back to the front room while she repacked the luggage. Just as she finished, the train pulled into Baltimore station. Martin jumped out of the coach before the train came to a full stop. From the window, I watched him as he spoke to a young man, and pointed toward our coach. The young man grabbed a cart. By the time we had fully stopped, he was entering the coach to retrieve our luggage.

"Ma'am," he said tipping his hat to us. "Your butler instructed me to handle your cases."

Miss Cameron pointed to our assembled luggage near the door. The young man set right to work, removing them from the coach. Miss Cameron stooped down to watch him out the window. While he stacked the luggage onto a cart, she checked her watch. Plato sat erect in between us. He too played his part well.

"By the time we are settled in, we will have ample time to dress for lunch. In the dining room, we can learn much from the other guests and the staff."

"How?"

"The Wartons are well known. We shouldn't have any trouble arranging a meeting as they will be quite anxious to meet a member of the English aristocracy." Miss

Cameron smiled at me. "Ah, the boy has finished with our cases." She motioned with her hand that I should proceed out the door.

On the station platform, Martin led us through the station to the street, where he had a carriage waiting for us. The luggage boy stacked the cases at the rear of the vehicle and then placed the smaller pieces on the luggage carrier atop the carriage. The drive to the hotel lasted a short while, and before I knew it, I was seated in a chair in the third floor suite in the Lord Baltimore Hotel. Martin and Miss Cameron unpacked and settled us in. Miss Cameron then turned her attention to me.

"I think the light blue silk for lunch and the afternoon tea," she said as she pulled the dress from the wardrobe.

When Miss Cameron had finished dressing me, I looked in the mirror. "That's me?" I whispered aloud.

Miss Cameron looked at me quizzically. "Yes, that is you."

"I think I look splendid for the first time in my life."

Miss Cameron opened her mouth as if to ask a question, but she stopped herself.

"Yes?" I said.

"Never mind. It's best that I know as little about you as possible."

I understood. It was the same reason given by the Olmsteds. It was best not to know people when one played a dangerous game. No real names were to be exchanged. I was Ellen Bennet, and no one else. That way, if, for some reason, we ran afoul of someone, Miss Cameron would not have to lie about my identity. She would know me only as Lady Ellen Bennet.

The conversation was interrupted by Martin's entrance.

"It is time for Lady Ellen to dine."

Miss Cameron nodded, picked up my shawl, then her own, and walked with me to the door, which Martin opened with a flourish. We walked out, down the hall and down the grand staircase. We made our way to the dining room.

"A table for Lady Ellen Bennet. There are two of us." Miss Cameron spoke to the Maitre'D at the entrance to the dining room.

"Yes ma'am," the Maitre'D said as he motioned for his assistant.

The assistant was young, with hair neatly combed smoothly front to back. In his hand he held two menus. He bowed to me slightly from the waist and then turned toward the dining room. "This way, if you will." We followed him to a table that was near the center of the room. When we were seated, Miss Cameron looked pleased. Whenever I looked around, I noted that complete strangers smiled and nodded to me. I returned the smile, and gave a very slight nod in response. I wanted to be reserved, as Martin had told me.

Soon the waiter came to take our order. I knew to order a substantial meal as lunch was considered the main meal of the day. As I ate the crowd around me turned their attention to a gentleman who entered the room. He was a tall, gray haired man dressed in a dark blue suit. The wait staff paid him prompt attention.

"Good afternoon, Mr Warton," said his waiter.

My ears tuned in while it took every once of my strength to not stare at the man. Miss Cameron played very cool indeed, by behaving as if she had not heard the name at all. Her example must be followed. While my heart raced at our good fortune, that the first person of our quest in Baltimore had shown up so quickly, my mind turned to the problem of how to make the man's acquaintance. He sat only a few feet away from us. The God above must have been on our side because no sooner had I thought of a silly way to meet Mr. Warton when a young woman, red haired, wearing a light blue dress with a skirt pushed out by hoops, flowed into the dining room. Every eye turned to watch her as she made her way to Mr. Warton's table.

"Papa," she said as he rose to pull the chair for her.

"Lavinia, I did not expect you so soon," Mr. Warton said as the young woman sat.

Since most eyes in the room were turned to her, mine would not be noticed if I too looked her way. She was elegant, and pretty. Not beautiful, in the classic sense, but sensitive in her face. Her porcelain skin reminded me of a doll I had seen once in a window of an antique shop in Trenton. Here I observed a past that I had seen represented on many television shows. Especially those produced by the BBC, the very programs that had taught me how to reproduce an English accent.

"What are you thinking?" Miss Cameron said.

"I have a plan."

From my purse I removed the handkerchief Mrs. Bishop had given me. The initials, EB, were beautifully embroidered on one end. Around the edges of the delicate linen was an even more refined lace. I left it on the table throughout our meal. When we had finished, I lightly wiped my forehead with this beautiful accessory. Keeping it in my hand, as we made our way out of the dining room, I dropped it near the Warton's table. And then I crossed my fingers that Miss Lavinia would find it. Miss Cameron and I then went to our suite. When the door was closed behind us, she smiled at me.

"Excellent." She removed her shawl. "Now I will nap until we hear from them."

"You think it will work?"

"You just wait, my dear." She disappeared into her room. I picked up the book I had been reading and curled up on the window seat. Plato curled up on the carpet below me. This habit, of the book and the dog, was the beginning of a beautiful routine we would share. We stayed in this manner until the knock came at the door.

Chapter Seven

Finding Marini

Martin opened the door to a young woman, of coffee and cream skin. In one hand she held the hanky. The other hand was poised to knock again. She was thin, elegant in bearing and wore her hair pulled tightly back into a bun at the base of her neck. She was dressed in a light blue dress, slightly expanded but without the hoops so fashionable in 1854. Over her dress was a stiffly starched white apron with dark blue trim. The apron had two pockets. Something about her face reminded me of Lavinia. Was this Lamentations' sister?

"I am to deliver these to Lady Ellen Bennet," she said in a voice that was pleasant and without any sort of accent.

"And you are?" Martin replied in his best butler voice.

"I am Maria, Miss Lavinia's personal maid."

We were not expecting the name of Maria. Martin, with his usual efficiency, stepped to the side. Maria entered. Seeing me, she made a curtsy. Plato sniffed at her feet. She showed no fear of him.

"You are Lady Ellen Bennet?"

"I am."

"Miss Lavinia sent me to return your handkerchief, and to give you this note." She reached into her pocket to pull out the envelope with the note.

Martin reached out to take the hanky and note. These he gave over to me. "Anything else?"

"I am to wait for a response," Maria said.

Martin brought the items to me.

"I am so glad it was found. It was something my mother gave to me." I took the hanky and placed it on the table next to the settee. I then opened the note, and read it. It was an invitation to tea at 5 pm. Here was luck! I went to the writing desk. I stopped short, realizing I had never written anything by the use of a stylus. In all my training on how to be a young lady, no one had thought to teach me about writing with such an instrument. How could they have known I had no such skill?

Martin, seeing my predicament, came to my rescue yet again. He pulled out paper from the desk drawer, and then dipped the stylus into the ink well. I took it. My first attempt was awful as the pressure that had to be applied when using a stylus is different from the use of a ball point pen. Even a modern fountain pen was easy to use compared to this. The first attempt had to be destroyed. The second attempt was much better, though not as lovely as the facsimiles I had seen in books. Or those hand written letters of old loving preserved in museums, as well as the note I had just read. Thankfully, I was a child and hoped my penmanship would would be seen in that light.

When finished, I started to fold the note, but Martin stopped me. "I will place it in an envelope for you, my lady." Martin blotted the note. He took an envelope out from the drawer. Next, he folded the note neatly and placed it in the envelope. This he handed to Maria.

"Thank you," Maria said, taking the note. She curtsied once more to me before taking her leave of us.

When the door shut, we waited a bit before speaking.

"Wake up Miss Cameron from her nap. We must plan," Martin said. "What time is tea?" he asked.

"Five o'clock."

Later, once Miss Cameron had revived herself, we sat in the drawing room.

"She said her name was Maria?"

"Yes," I said. Martin nodded.

"I should have stayed up."

"Why, do you know what Marini looks like?" Martin said.

"I think it's her," I said. "It must be."

"You sound very sure of it." Miss Cameron studied my face.

"She looks like Miss Lavinia."

"Ja, the same father. From the mother of Lamentations."

"Botlieb, please, think of the age of our young charge here."

"Miss Cameron, Lady Bennet, Ell, she is old enough to know these things if she is old enough to play such a dangerous game as we play."

"I hadn't thought of it that way." Miss Cameron leaned back into the chair.

"Would you please explain things to me? What has Marini to do with Lavinia other than be her maid?"

When I look back on this moment, I see that neither Martin nor Miss Cameron had the desire to spell things out for me. The one looked at the other, hoping to be relieved of the duty of telling an eleven year old girl the facts of life as lived by the men and women of the pre-civil War South. After a few moments of this silence and hesitation, Martin cleared his throat.

"You see, Ell," Martin paused, searching for the best words.

"I'll do it, but you must leave, Botlieb."

Martin hesitated, then left the room.

Miss Cameron moved to the settee. "Come, sit next to me." She patted the seat. She then sat back, took a deep breath, pushed it out so that her cheeks puffed out. She then spoke, slowly, deliberately. "It is a disgusting practice, but among the slave owning men, sometimes they use their female slaves as companions for the night."

"You mean, they have sex with them?"

Miss Cameron was startled. It took her a few moments to collect herself. Finally, she spoke. "Yes. It is part of the ugly practice of slavery."

"They don't tell you about this in school."

"Perhaps they should? I mean, I forget myself. It is not a subject to be discussed at great length. By children or by ladies, certainly. Sufficient to say, it is why we must destroy slavery in the United States. The mixing of the races, as well as the demeaning posture it places the women in, both black and white, why, it is sickening all round. Do you understand?"

"Yes, Miss Cameron, I do. We must be sensitive to it. Not say out loud what we know?"

Miss Cameron studied me for what must have been a full minute. Then she said, "You have a maturity beyond your years. Even beyond what the most sophisticated young woman would dare to mention, let along speak of."

The clock chimed four o'clock. Miss Cameron stood.

"Come. We must prepare ourselves for tea. Botlieb?"

Martin returned to the parlor from his bedroom.

"I have thought what we must do," he said as soon as he entered. "To make certain of this Maria, Lamentations must see her." Martin looked to Miss Cameron. "Can you, through your people, get a message to Moses?"

"I can." Miss Cameron stood. She looked to me. "You should not attend that tea without me. But I may not have returned in time."

"Where are you going?"

"Never mind that, young lady. Martin, you will have to attend her if I am not back." Martin nodded. "It will seem irregular, but it must be so. Make the time honored excuse of a headache. Or whatever excuse you deem appropriate."

"I will," Martin replied.

Miss Cameron picked up her hat, crossed to the mirrored hall table, and set it on her head. She spoke as she arranged it, tying her ribbons with emphasis on her words. "Do act your part *well*, Lady Bennet. We can have no mistakes from this point forward. We want the Warton's to feel secure and honored to have *you* as their guest. That will distract them from what is going on in their background." She turned to face us. "That is what their slaves are, a background. Human beings that are not noticed as such." She picked up her parasol. "And now, I leave you. It is just after four. I hope to be back in time for tea." She crossed to the door. Martin opened it for her.

Once the door shut behind her, the two of us stood motionless for a while. We were thinking about our mission at hand, and that our expert in all things social had just left us to our own inventions.

"I believe you have a tea frock?" Martin turned toward me.

The tea frock was hanging on the front of the wardrobe door, for Miss Cameron had anticipated the tea date. I recalled the fitting of the dress, so was assured I could put it on correctly. It was the hair that puzzled me. I looked in the mirror. It would pass, but the ribbons were wrong. The tea dress had pink ribbons intertwined through the blouse. There were pink ribbons on the dressing table. I supposed these ribbons were to replace the blue ones currently in my hair. I wondered, if in all the tricks and resources Martin had at hand, could he braid my hair using the pink ribbons instead of the blue ones now intertwined in it?

Martin proved adept at braiding hair. The ribbons, however, were another matter. I decided to tie them at the bottom of my braids, to allow their length to spill down my back.

I hated the look of it. I yanked them out. I took a pair of scissors and cut the one ribbon in half. These shorter lengths proved more manageable and prettier. Martin managed to turn each ribbon into a nice, asymmetrical bow. I looked myself over once more. My new look, the dark hair especially, proved attractive. I added a bit of pomade to keep my hair sleek.

The white tea frock was a lovely dress, its lace trim added the look of wealth to an otherwise simple garment.

In later years I would think of the dress as one of the most elegant I had ever worn throughout my days as a time traveler. I wanted Mrs. Cowell to make all my clothes, her work was so exemplary, every seam straight and finished. Mrs. Cowell understood how a lady should look, but beyond that, Mrs. Cowell understood that it was the quality of what she wore that was as important to a lady.

A lady. I had never thought of myself in those terms before. In 1974, only my grandmother might mention the word. To my mother, I was a girl who would grow into a woman. Boys and men were a thing of the future. No training was needed. Dad would clue me in when the time came. And yet, here I was, nearly twelve years old, thrust into a past that referred to a girl as a young lady, and I had no reference point to go on. Here was another thing I needed to know and understand if I was to be a time traveler. Then there was the problem of not knowing who the girl in the mirror truly was. The frightening thing was that I knew her but didn't know her. I longed to speak to the Old Man. Only he, I was convinced, could help me make sense of what had happened to me. I turned away from my image. I returned to the drawing room.

"Well, now we are a true lady," Martin said to me.

"Do you think this will work?"

Martin checked his watch. "It's nearly five. Shall we go?"

"What about Miss Cameron?"

"There is nothing to be done. Perhaps she returns in a few minutes, but you mustn't be late. You are a well brought up English lady. Remember?"

I nodded my head. Martin placed his hand on the door knob. "What is my name?"

"Your name? Oh, you are Botlieb, my butler, from Munich."

Martin bowed slightly at the waist as he opened the door. Once I had passed through, he took a look around the room, and the hallway before shutting and locking our door. He then followed me a pace behind as I walked to the stairwell. In the tea room, I strolled to the Warton's table. Martin slowed his pace to stand a few feet away as Mr. Warton stood and pulled the chair for me. He bowed as I came near.

"Lady Ellen Bennet, I am George Warton."

"Mr. Warton," I said, giving a slight bow of my head. I took my seat.

Martin gave a slight bow to Mr. Warton before stepping back to the wall.

"This is my daughter, Miss Lavinia."

Lavinia gave me a bow of her head, which I returned.

"Lady Bennet, may I introduce Sir John Symington-Reed, and Mr. Samuel Hawkins."

The men stood. I repeated my nodding from my chair. Sir John and Mr. Hawkins gave me a slight bow before returning to their seats.

The servers laid the tea things on the table. Trays of sandwiches and cakes, biscuits and fruits were placed before us. Jams and butters, nestled in silver bowls, spread out across the table. The tea was served from beautiful pots, its contents poured into white china cups. We dipped highly polished teaspoons of silver into the tea to stir our creams and sugars. We used highly polished silver knives to butter our biscuits, and then lavish them with the fresh jams. This, I realized, was how the rich lived in 1854. But in

1974, nearly any family, save for the very poor, could afford such a tea spread. Therefore, I did not have to pretend to be used to such things as tea. Though I did not care for the beverage, the food pleased me. I wished for my hot beverage of choice. A cup of hot chocolate on a snowy afternoon in Trenton was always a pleasing activity. Specially accompanied by my mother's coconut cake or her scones fresh from the oven.

I missed my mother. She, who had not believed me, indulged my fancies of time travel. Except that now it was not fanciful thinking. Not on my part. What was that saying I had heard so many times? Be careful for what you wish for?

"How do you find our part of the country, Lady Bennet," Mr. Warton asked.

"I find it quite lovely, Mr. Warton."

"I understand you are from Derby?" Sir John asked the question.

"Born there, yes, Sir Symington-Reed. However, since my parent's death, I've not been back."

"I am sorry to hear of it, and you must call me Sir John."

"Thank you, Sir John."

"How long have you been an orphan?" Mr. Hawkins asked.

"For nearly eight years."

"Please, gentlemen, shall we speak of brighter things?" Lavinia nearly demanded.

"Indeed we shall," Sir John said.

"We have a new foal I think you'll appreciate, Mr. Hawkins." As he spoke, Mr. Warton neatly arranged the sandwiches on his plate.

"Is that so?" Mr. Hawkins had a deep southern accent.

"She's a beautiful thing," Lavinia said. "Red as mahogany with three white stockings and a stripe down the length of her face." She turned to me. "Do you like horses, Lady Bennet?"

"I do."

"Why you must come and ride out at our place," Mr. Warton said.

"It will be my pleasure to do so." I smiled. I then noted that Sir John scrutinized me a bit too much. It would be my luck to have to perform my best English accent and mannerism with a real Englishman as my audience. Nothing to do at that moment except do my best. "I am afraid I have no riding habit with me."

Just then we were joined by Miss Cameron. Inwardly, I sighed in relief. As was usual, the formalities were observed as the men stood until she was seated.

"Please do forgive, but I was called away." She then looked directly at me. "Your aunt has been notified that we have arrived safely."

I picked up the cue. "It was entirely my fault. Aunt told me to write as soon as I arrived. I missed the early afternoon mail."

"I sent a telegraph." Miss Cameron smiled.

"A modern woman," Sir John said. Miss Cameron gave a slight nod of her head in acknowledgement of the compliment.

"We have invited Lady Bennet to Split Oaks Plantation, " Lavinia said to Miss Cameron. "I hope I've not overstepped myself."

"Is that your home?"

"It is. We would love you to come and ride, and attend my wedding."

"Oh, indeed." Miss Cameron turned to me. "We will advise your aunt of this change in plans, though I dare say it will be welcomed as a part of your discovery of this part of the country."

"Oh yes, of course!" Mr. Warton now spoke. "Come and see how the gentle folk live in the South. I dare say, with pride I do not think lacks warrant, that we live the gentile life somewhat better than the Yankees. No offense Miss Cameron."

"No offense taken, Mr. Warton. I have heard of this Southern pride in your good manners and polite living. As yet, I have not been disappointed." Miss Cameron smiled.

Mr. Warton paused. He too had detected the ever-so-slight sarcasm in Miss Cameron's voice. He remained calm, smiled at her. "As soon as Mr. Ewell arrives," now his glance shifted to me, "I insist we all travel down together."

"Mr. Ewell" I asked.

"Mr. Ewell is my betrothed." Lavinia smiled.

"Ah."

Sir John had returned his scrutiny to me. Miss Cameron noted it.

"A wedding and riding, we may have to visit the dressmaker for a riding habit."

"If I am not too forward, I have riding habits that would fit Lady Bennet." Lavinia seemed a gracious person. Yet, she owned slaves. My mind could not help but question how a woman who could be so kind to a stranger, could also be so thoughtless as to own another human being. It was difficult for me to reconcile the two sides of her.

"That is very generous of you, Miss Lavinia." Miss Cameron smiled broadly. She played her part well.

What I could not see was that Gannon had entered the dinning room. Fortunately, I had my back to him. Martin saw him. He guessed who he was. The first I knew that danger was afoot was when Mr. Warton, who sat to my left, turned to him and motioned for him to come to the table. Lavinia then glanced to see who her father motioned to. Immediately her face turned red. She jerked her head back to her father.

"Please, not here." she said, with a certain edge to her voice.

Mr. Warton looked hard on his daughter, but then lifted his hand to indicate the person was to halt. I wanted to look around in the worst way, but I knew that would be considered impolite. So I focused on the delicious cake on my plate as a way to keep me in my place. Martin came into my view. The way he looked at me spoke of the danger I was in. Miss Cameron looked to Martin as well. Mr. Warton then excused himself from the table. He and Gannon-Martin told me this years later-went into the bar. Those of us at table then resumed our talk of Lavinia's wedding, which was to take place at Split Oaks on the following Saturday. Today was Tuesday. I wondered where Mrs. Tubman was, and from what point she would leave Maryland to lead her group to Philadelphia. It was a good thing not to know. "Let them find *you*," Miss Cameron had said about the individuals involved in the Underground Railroad.

Martin then approached me and Miss Cameron. "Miss Cameron, it is the hour you requested for Lady Ellen's rest," was all he said.

Miss Cameron stood. She spoke directly to Lavinia. "Thank you for your hospitality."

"It has been a pleasure, Miss Lavinia." I gave a slight nod of the head, smiled to the gentlemen, and then left the tea room, Miss Cameron and Martin discreetly trailing behind me.

Looking back on this episode of my life, I don't think any of this would have been pulled off without Martin there to help me. It should be said he helped *us,* for he watched over Miss Cameron as well. Before we entered our room, as was his habit, Martin looked up and down the hall to ensure that we had not been followed. He locked the door securely after we entered. Plato, who usually would greet us, stayed seated at Miss Cameron's bedroom door.

"Why are the drapes drawn?" I asked.

"You will soon see. First, call the dog to you."

"Plato, come here." He still had a limp but he could now move quite well. He sat next to me when I sat in the chair.

Miss Cameron opened the door to her bedroom. "Say nothing." She said it directly to me, but then looked to Martin as well. She turned back toward her room. "You may come out now." Out walked Lamentations.

Here was a surprise. Though I would have given him another one of my hugs, I kept to the script of our little drama. "How nice to see you, and see that you are well," I said, still using my English accent. I didn't want to relax one bit until we were all out of danger.

"I am fine, Miss, I mean, Lady Ellen. Just fine. I heard you done meet my sister. Or you think you did. Miss Cameron here says I need to see her, to identify her."

"Yes, but how we should do that, I don't know." I smiled weakly.

"We've been invited to Split Oaks, for the wedding."

"We can't let it go that far," Lamentations said.

"Why not?" Martin asked.

"Split Oaks is down in St. Charles County. That just means further to go. We here, close to New Jersey and Pennsylvania."

"We'll need to make excuses," Miss Cameron spoke.

"The aunt will deny her permission," Martin said.

"First," I chimed in, "we have to see if it's Marini or not." I turned to Lamentations. "She calls herself Maria."

"Yes, that's right. That's Mr. Warton's doing. He gives out them Roman and Italian names to his slaves. Was our mother named her Marini. It's a name that was in her family for generations."

"What does she look like?" I asked.

"I haven't seen her for awhile, but she was always a skinny girl. Mama said she would be tall. Has she gotten tall?"

"She has."

"We still need a visual confirmation," Miss Cameron said.

Just then a knock was heard at the door. Plato stood, wagged his tail. Miss Cameron motioned for Lamentations to return to her room. When the door was shut, Martin answered the door. It was Marini. She wasn't, however, alone in the hall. In back of her, at a few feet distance was Vigilis, standing erect, as if at attention. I immediately grabbed Plato by the neck to moves us out of his sightline.

"Yes?" Martin said with all his expert seriousness.

"I am here to deliver a formal invitation to Lady Bennet," Marini said.

Martin held out his hand to receive the invitation. Marini was about to give it to him when I spoke up.

"Come in, Maria, and wait for my reply."

Marini looked around the door to see me standing by the writing desk. She stepped into the door. Vigilis attempted to peer around to see who spoke.

"You wait there," Marini said with authority.

Martin closed the door behind Marini. She walked across the room to where I stood, curtsied and then handed me an envelope. I opened it. Inside was the engraved invitation to Lavinia's wedding. It was beautiful, like no invitation I had ever seen. The paper was thick and textured. The font was elegant. The border around the wording was a graceful and exquisite twisting of lines that looked like vines. At that moment I was sorely disappointed that I would not attend such a magnificent event as the invitation promised. I sat at the desk to write a note.

"Dear Miss Lavinia," I began. "I have in hand your beautiful invitation. At this time, I cannot answer yay or nay to my attendance as I must inform my aunt of this momentous event and visit. I shall have Miss Cameron send another telegraph to her forthwith. Please have patience, your obedient servant, Lady Ellen Bennet."

"Maria?" I spoke as I blotted the writing. "I wonder if you would be so kind as to see a dress I think would be appropriate for Miss Lavinia's nuptials."

"I am sure anything you would wear would be fine, Lady Bennet."

"It would ease my mind to have you see it."

Miss Cameron and Martin understood what I was up to. Martin went to the door and ever so silently locked it. Miss Cameron crossed to the door of her room. She opened it and eased herself inside, but did not close it all the way. When I had finished blotting and folding, I handed the envelope to Marini. She took it and placed it in the pocket of her apron.

She followed me to the door of my room. Lamentations, who stood in the shadows of Miss Cameron's room, saw her pass.

"Marini?" he called in a whisper.

Marini knew the voice. She stopped dead, and then turned towards it. The door opened wider and out came the older brother to have the sister run into his arms. Both of them, understanding the dangerous situation they were in, whispered into one another's ears, and wept silently.

"We have our confirmation," I said to Miss Cameron.

The three of us waited patiently for a few minutes for the two to have their moment of brotherly and sisterly affection. But soon Miss Cameron intervened for if Marini stayed too long she might arouse suspicion.

"I come to take you away," Lamentations said to Marini.

"Take me where?"

"Away from slavery, girl, to freedom."

"I can't do that."

"Why not?"

"Miss Lavinia is getting married, and we are moving to Georgia."

"Once you in Georgia, you ain't never gonna taste freedom."

"I have a nice life now, Lam. I am Miss Lavinia's personal maid. No outdoor work at all. No kitchen work. Just combing her hair and helping her to dress, and doing like I'm doing now." Marini took out her hanky and wiped her eyes.

"When she say jump, you jump and hope you jump high enough. If you don't jump high enough, she can sell you whenever she want."

"Listen to me, Lam. I found something out about Miss Lavinia and me. It's important, so you listen." She sat with him on the settee, holding his hands as much to control the emotions as with affection. "Remember how mama would never say who my father is? Well, I found out. And it's like this, Lam. Miss Lavinia, she is my sister."

Lamentations sat silently. No one, not any of us, had expected such a revelation.

"And that boy standing in the hall. That is George Warton's only son. And my brother."

"From our mama?"

"No. From our cousin, Stella."

I could see the anger well up in Lamentations eyes, and then course down to his body. Martin saw it as well.

"He works with Gannon and they are looking for you, Lam. Mr. Warton wants you back. Gannon will make five thousand dollars if he can bring you back. And Vigilis will take twenty per cent. And Mr. Warton has promised Vigilis his freedom when he is twenty-one."

"I will kill that man," Lamentations said as he rose up to his full height.

Martin crossed to him.

"You must keep your voice down."

"Marini, you must go." Miss Cameron said.

"Yes ma'am, I will." She looked at all of us and then said, "Don't worry, I won't say anything." She turned to me. "I will use the dress as an excuse, of you showing it to me." She curtsied again to me, crossed to the door and opened it. "Let's go," we heard her say to Vigilis.

Martin closed the door behind her. The four of us stood stunned into silence.

"I have to go," Lamentations said.

"Not until the night," Martin said. "We must have darkness as your cover."

"I have to talk to her. Talk her out of this life she thinks she has."

"You can't do that. You cannot risk yourself, Mrs. Tubman or us." Miss Cameron said.

"She doesn't know what she's doing."

"That is not for us to decide. We can only offer her freedom. We cannot make her take it. And as much as we may hate to admit it, the one freedom she does have is the freedom to decide." Miss Cameron turned to Martin. "Please, will you get the sherry from my room," she said as she fanned herself vigorously.

"But why wouldn't she want her freedom?" I asked.

"Fear, mostly. If she were caught trying to run away, her punishment would be quite severe. Just as Lamentations punishment would be if he is caught."

Martin returned with the bottle of sherry. He poured us all a shot in the cut crystal glasses on the sideboard of our suite. I was given half as much. Miss Cameron downed hers in one gulp. She held her glass out for a second shot. Lamentations held his in his hand without drinking it. He was too busy thinking. I sipped mine.

"You are her brother, but you promise a difficult and treacherous journey to a life that has no allure for her." Martin now spoke. "Her sister promises a life of work that is not difficult. The question is, does Miss Lavinia know that Marini is her sister?"

"That might make a difference." Miss Cameron said.

"Why?" I asked.

"Because she could find it repugnant that her father slept with a slave. And the issue of that encounter is Marini."

"Many of them know, but they pretend they don't." Lamentations took a sip of his sherry. "The missus suffered plenty before she died. Warton slept more with his slave women than with his wife. Now I learn our mama and cousin Stella were a part of his stable."

The way Lamentations said the word, *stable*, made me shudder.

"The wives know. But do the daughters as well?" Miss Cameron sighed.

"Then," I said slowly, "we must tell Miss Lavinia."

"That is a huge responsibility, Lady Ellen. For how can we know the consequences of such information?" Miss Cameron downed her second glass of sherry.

"Lady Ellen Bennet is used to risk," Martin said.

"If you are about to tell me something of her, please don't." Miss Cameron held out her glass. Martin filled it.

"I will not say a word more." Martin glanced at me. "Lamentations, you will return to your hiding tonight. Tomorrow, we will have an answer for you regarding your sister." Martin then went into the sideboard where he retrieved a set of cards. "Poker anyone?"

It was on this night that I learned the game that would stay with me for the rest of my life. It helped to while away the time, and helped in other instances as well. Martin cleared off the small table. Lamentations set up the chairs. The four of us sat, the cards and decanter of sherry in the center of the table. Some might think the adults were about to corrupt a girl. I think of it as the time I learned an invaluable skill needed to practice the art of time travel.

Chapter Eight

The Plan is Saved

I couldn't sleep. Marini's face kept staring at me through the dark. Her eyes were desperate. Confused.

Or was it me who was confused?

That Marini loved both her brothers, there were no doubts. That she liked the life she led is what unsettled me. How could anyone like their slavery? Why wouldn't she jump at the chance to leave it all behind her, even if it meant some insecurity? Wouldn't her brother, Lamentations, see to her survival?

My trouble was that I asked the questions of a modern girl. In the middle of 1854 Baltimore, this modern girl could see only the glories of freedom. Later, much later, after I had read volumes of books on slavery, from the time of the Romans to the twentieth century, only then would there be an understanding on my part. In the years to come, I would see that Lamentations offered her freedom, yes, but at a price. His freedom was not free. For Marini, that price was the danger of the journey, plus no guarantees that they would arrive safely at their destination. What Marini had now was a certain protection afforded her by her father.

I wanted so to persuade her to take this awful risk. That was my mission, the very reason I had come to Baltimore. Inside my head, I searched for the right words to encourage her. Was there some magic I could work to give her the desire to follow Lamentations and Mrs. Tubman? What would change her mind?

A muffled sound came from the sitting room. Plato, who now slept on my bed, pricked up his ears. I sat up to listen. A sound like a window opening lured me out of bed.

"Stay." It was a hoarse whisper to Plato. He kept his head up, but stayed on the bed. He watched me intently as I left the room.   In the sitting room, Lamentations stepped out of the window to slide down a rope. When he had disappeared, I ran in on my tiptoes to see where he had gone. At the window, I peeked out from the corner. Lamentations was no where to be seen. I stepped in front of the window to get a better look. Still no Lamentations. My next move was to lean out the window.

"I wouldn't do that."

It was Martin's voice. I stopped.

"I want to know that he's okay."

"*Okay* is not a nineteenth century word, yes?" Martin smiled at me.

"Yes."

"You are to know nothing until you need to know. Understand?"

"Yes."

"Good." Martin poured himself a drink from a pretty decanter I had not seen before. He poured a second one, and held that glass out to me. "To help you sleep, yes?"

"Yes." It tasted sweet yet strong. "What is it?"

"It's like a sherry, but from Portugal, so it is called Port."

"I like it." We sipped our Port in silence. After a while, the effect of the liquor turned me warm and lazy. I sat in the large chair near the window Lamentations had slipped out of. For the first time in days, I felt content, without pressure. I leaned back in the chair. Out of the corner of my eye I saw something move through the yard below me. I leaned forward to see what it was. But nothing moved now. "Is that a maze?" I asked.

"It is." Martin joined me at the window. "Tomorrow you can try your luck in it."

"Yes, I'll do that." I was back to leaning against the comfort of the chair. My eyes closed of their own will, not mine. Martin's footsteps approached me.

"My lady needs her sleep." I heard him place his glass on the table nearby. "Come along." His arms reached under me and I felt myself picked up.

"Is he alright?"

"He is."

Martin placed me on my bed. He drew the covers over me. I felt Plato curl up next to me.

"Thank you Martin."

"Sleep."

I did. In the morning the sun streamed through the window. Plato lay stretched out on the floor in a patch of sunlight. When the clock in the other room chimed seven, we both got up. In the sitting room, no one was about. I knocked on Miss Cameron's door. There was no answer. Nor did Martin answer his door. I was alone in the suite. Back in the sitting room I noticed the breakfast left on the sideboard. There were eggs, biscuits and sauces. I was about to help myself when I noticed a note had been left for me. I opened it. It was from Miss Cameron.

"Lady Ellen, please wait for me before venturing out. I should return around nine. Do have your breakfast. Miss Cameron. PS, we have fed and walked Plato."

I helped myself to generous portions of the food. I sat on the chair by the window to eat. Below, ground keepers busied themselves with trimming the tall shrubs that held the maze's secrets. From the height of my sitting position, I could see a part of the inner path system of the maze. The many paths formed a puzzle that invited the curious to come and try their luck. The urge to try my luck in this tangled web got the better of me. After eating, I dressed. My hair was not very neat, but was passable. If any one of importance saw me, the explanation would be the morning's exercise had disheveled me.

"Plato, you stay here. I can't risk Gannon seeing you."

I ran down the stairs. On the ground floor I maintained a bit of decorum through the lobby and out to the back veranda. It was then I saw Marini head into the maze. Now was my chance to speak to her.

Without any caution I ran across the lawn, then followed her through the maze's entrance. Once inside, I turned left. After coming round the first bend, a dead end was in sight. I retraced my steps. I took a right into the first opening after the entrance. This path, with its two jig-jag turns, went nearly around the entire maze. Another dead end soon halted my progress. Back I went. I came to a fork, took it to the right, and was stuck again. That's when the voices were heard coming from the center of the maze. First a woman spoke, followed by a man. The voices were rather loud. They were arguing.

I turned around to retrace my steps. This time, at the fork, taking the left I found my way back to the entrance. From that point, I went the opposite direction inside the maze. For a moment, the voices were lost. I decided to cheat. At a thin place in the wall of the hedge, I forced my way through the bushes. Faintly, the voices returned. I wandered around a bend which did not end. At another fork, the first path went nowhere. The second brought me closer to my goal. The voices were louder. Another wrong turn forced me back, but the second one brought me closer.

After a few moments I had reached the sixth inner circle. The voices were now clear. I then found the seventh circle. I stopped. The woman's voice belonged to Lavinia. I pushed ahead to the eighth circle. At the entrance to this path, I glanced to my right. There, half hidden by the curve in the shrubbery, was Marini. She was eavesdropping.

My first impulse was to go to her, to listen to what she was listening to. I took a step in that direction, but stopped myself. Best not surprise her, and best to allow her to think she was unobserved. I carefully stepped toward the ninth circle. Here, the entrance to the heart of the maze was plainly visible. I looked for my own place of concealment. Another thinning of the bushes allowed me to squeeze through to the perfect hiding place where I could peek through the bushes to see the entrance to the middle. Here I could see Lavinia seated on a bench. A man stood to her right, his arms crossed behind him. As he listened to Lavinia, he seemed impatient.

"Father promised. And now you say he lies?" Lavinia spoke.

"No, my dear, I say he is confused as to the terms of our contract." The man spoke with a much deeper Southern drawl than Lavinia did.

"But my household is set up, Edward, everything's in place."

"Lavinia, dearest," he squatted in front of her so that he could look her in the eyes. "I do not need these extra house servants."

"Maria will be useful once we have children."

"Our Ewell mammy will see to their care, just like she has done for the last 30 years."

"Kathy is growing old."

"Kathy has her daughter, who I promised would one day take her mother's place."

"I am weary of this argument, Edward. And I still do not understand why Maria and Vigilis are not wanted."

Edward sighed. He took the seat next to Lavinia. He started to speak but then stopped himself. His face became studied like any face in deep thought.

"Well, Edward?" Lavinia sounded impatient.

Edward took a deep breath. "I look for words to convey the right meaning with as much *sensitivity* as possible. Yet, what I have to say to you, the startling truth is harsh, no matter how I phrase it. But the truth shall be known."

"And that is?"

"The Ewells do not mix with their *property*."

"What does that mean?" Lavinia sounded harsh.

"Men of the white race do not mix with women of the black."

The shock was as clear as day on Lavinia's face. She stood up, violently shaken by what Edward had said to her.

"What do you mean by that?" she said with a hiss.

"By god, woman, don't you know? Has your father's escapades to his house servants' quarters escaped you?"

Lavinia slapped Edward. Hard. She raised her hand to strike him again, but he caught it by the forearm.

"The truth shall set you free, is what I have been told." Lavinia attempted to free herself. "No, dearest," his voice was calm as he spoke, "you shall hear it. All of it."

Lavinia squirmed in Edward's grasp. "Your maid is your half- sister."

"No!"

"And that boy who runs around the country looking for runaway slaves with that man Gannon? Your half-brother."

Lavinia groaned, twisted her arm.

"Oh, yes, in your heart you knew it, didn't you?" He took Lavinia's other arm, forcing her to face him. She burst into tears. "Ah, sweet lady," he reached into his pocket for his handkerchief, "cry it out." He wiped the tears as they came down her face. "It won't change a thing, but it will relieve you."

"You're a cruel man."

Edward shook his head. "I reckon you now understand why we have our rules at Cotton Wood. As Mrs. Ewell, you will *never* have to wonder where your husband sleeps. And our children will *never* have to say they have brothers and sisters who are slaves."

Lavinia groaned again. Edward comforted her. He guided her to her seat on the bench, sat next to her. He continued to wipe her tears. After a few moments, Lavinia calmed herself.

"What do I tell Maria?"

"The truth."

After some hesitation, Lavinia nodded her head.

"And Papa?"

"I will speak to him." Edward returned to his standing position with his arms crossed in back. "We could sell them, if they are indeed your property. With that money you can purchase another young girl to *your* liking."

"Vigilis belongs to Papa."

The eavesdropping Marini surely heard this conversation. If the truth would set anyone free, as Edward put it, it had now set her free. For there was no future with Lavinia. Her life, as she had imagined it, was shattered, and her future unknowable. Perhaps now the journey north with Lamentations and Mrs. Tubman made sense to her, perhaps now the risk was worth taking.

Edward checked his pocket watch. "Come my dearest, let us get ourselves some breakfast."

Lavinia smiled at Edward. He helped her to stand, and then she took his arm. They turned toward where I stood. I backed away from the hedge. I could see their feet as they walked passed me. When the crunching of the gravel grew fainter, I negotiated the thinning bush out onto the other side. I ran to where I hoped Marini would still be. She was there. She stood without moving, staring down at the ground. She looked up at me, started to speak, but instead shook her head. She started to run around me, but I stopped her.

"No! Stay here until you know they are inside the hotel."

"They will miss me, will want to know where I am."

"You stay here. I will see to it that they go directly to the dining room." I then ran back through the maze. I took one wrong turn, which ate up valuable seconds, but finally I found the correct path. Luck smiled on me for a second time that morning as the two were involved in a conversation with Sir John right outside the maze. I straightened my hair as best I could, and then approached them.

"Good morning, Miss Lavinia," I said with my cheeriest disposition. Lavinia's eyes were red and puffy.

"Good morning, Lady Bennet. Please, allow me to introduce you to my fiancé, Edward Ewell."

"Lady Bennet," Edward said, tipping his hat to me.

"Mr. Ewell," I said with my curtsy. I then turned to Sir John. "Sir John," I said with a slight nod of my head.

"Lady Bennet," he said as he too tipped his hat.

"I am famished," I said. "And I am afraid I have been awfully naughty, running out for exercise without anyone at my side. If Miss Cameron finds out, I shall be lectured without mercy."

"We shall say you were with us," Lavinia said. She took my hand. "Now, shall we all go to breakfast?"

The four of us went into the dinning room. Though the prospect of eating a second large meal somewhat dismayed me, to protect Marini I was willing to eat the side of a mountain.

"Have you tried your luck with the maze, my lady?" Sir John asked.

"I did this morning, but after the third time of being terribly lost, I gave it up and walked around the grounds instead."

"Hmmm, I thought I saw you coming out of the maze," Sir John said.

"I peeked in, walked a few more paces, to see if I could solve its mystery. But I thought better of it."

"A wise decision." Edward smiled at me. "Miss Warton and I used one of the ground's keepers to show us the way. I suggest you do the same."

"I will."

The conversation then turned to the upcoming nuptials. Lavinia asked me if I had heard anything yet from my aunt. I shook my head. I glanced up at the clock. It was nine. Surely Marini had time to return to her room.

"You seem a bit anxious," Sir John said to me.

"I don't wish Miss Cameron to be anxious, to wonder where I am."

"Send up a note." Sir John motioned for the waiter.

"You are kind, Sir John."

The waiter was instructed to bring note paper and a stylus. My note was simple. I wrote, "Here in the dining room with Miss Lavinia, her fiancé, and Sir John." The waiter gave the note to a bellboy who immediately went to deliver it.

"How long have you been residing in the United States?" Sir John smiled at me.

"It seems like forever, but I came here when I was a child of four."

"You have lived here longer than you have in England." Sir John sipped his tea. "That explains the strange accent."

"Strange? Yes, I suppose so." I did not question him further because I didn't know what to say.

"Do you remember your parents at all?" Lavinia asked.

"Vaguely." I shut my eyes as if to remember. Truth was I couldn't remember my own parents. Instead of my dad, another man's face popped into my brain. This was a man with jet black hair and very pale skin, with dark blue eyes that bored into my soul. I felt strong emotions well up inside me. For the first time since coming back to 1854, I felt awfully confused. Tears were welling in my eyes. My heart began to race. I looked around the table. Lavinia looked at me with concern. Edward reached for his handkerchief. Sir John scrutinized my face. "Sorry," I said in a hoarse whisper. I pushed my chair back. "Sorry," I repeated as I stood up. I then walked rapidly away.

When I came to the stairway, I ran up the stairs not caring at all about what anyone thought of me. Breathless at the third floor, I turned down the hall towards our suite. There, standing outside my door was Vigilis. I slowed down as I approached.

"I saw you in Philadelphia," he said to me.

"You are mistaken."

"No I ain't. And don't tell me you must look like someone else."

I stopped still, wiped my tears. Sooner or later I would have to deal with Vigilis. Might as well be now.

"And if I was?"

"I think you know where Lamentations is."

"Who is that?"

Vigilis scoffed. He started to approach me, but thought better of it. No matter what or who I was, I was still a free born white girl and he was a young man born into slavery. Looking back on this episode I could see he was being brave just to question me. He stood and faced me squarely.

"Look here. I can get you a fat reward if you will tell me where Lamentations is."

"Why would I be interested in your reward? Do you think money is any concern to me?"

Vigilis scoffed again. "I know your sort. There is never enough money."

There was no answer from me because I didn't know what to say. Without a word further, I walked to my door and opened it.

"One more thing. I think you be getting my sister into trouble."

Fear shot through me. Without turning back to look at Vigilis, I said, "I would never do anything to harm her." I entered the suite, and then shut the door in Vigilis' face.

What Vigilis said had truth in it. Marini, if caught running away, would be severely punished, or sold. Had not Mrs. Tubman warned us of the dangers we all faced? Especially the escaped slaves. If Marini did not want to take this risk, who was I to encourage it?

"Here you are." Miss Cameron faced me.

"I'm sorry. I disobeyed you."

"My. We are admitting it and apologizing for it?" Miss Cameron leaned down to study my face. "What has happened?"

"Vigilis, Marini's brother is standing out in the hall. He accused me of harming her."

"Why would he say that?"

"He knows it was me in Philadelphia. He'll tell Gannon."

"I am of the opinion that we need to move forward with this plan." Miss Cameron walked into the sitting room. She sat down at the desk, took out paper from the drawer. I followed her. "Do you know where Botlieb is?"

"No."

"Then I will need you to take this note."

"Who do I take it to?

"You take it to the garden, and leave it under bench in the center of the labyrinth."

"Under the bench?"

"Yes. You will have to dig a little hole, hide it in the hole, and then cover it up with the gravel. Make it look as if nothing is there." She fell silent as she wrote the note. I peered over her shoulder. What she wrote did not make sense to me. "It's in Latin," she said. "And even if you could read Latin, the message would not be meaningful to you." She blotted the note. "Once you have found the center-

"I know how to get there."

"Ah, that is where you were this morning. Listening in?"

"How do you know this?"

"Never mind that. As you travel through the labyrinth, be aware of others. Once you bury the note, you can find a place to hide and watch the area until the note is taken."

"How long will I have to wait?"

"I don't know. The site is checked often but not on a regular schedule." She handed me the note. "Take Plato, he could use the exercise and he is an excellent excuse for lingering."

"I think we should look to see if Vigilis is still in the hall. If he sees the dog, he will be certain of me."

Miss Cameron opened the door to peek out. Seeing no one, she opened it enough for us to leave. I shoved the note into my small purse. Instead of walking down to the main staircase, I turned left to use the servants back stairs. Before entering, I listened. All was silent. On the way down I met no one. On the ground floor, the stair door opened out onto the kitchen side of the veranda in back of the hotel. I walked out and across. Many guests were seated there, some drinking tea, most engaged in conversations. Others read books. One man admired Plato. Others looked out to gaze at the garden. It was early fall. The flowers still bloomed. I ran down the steps, and across the lawn. The maze was to my left. It did not take me long to find the old path to the center. Plato found it great fun, sniffing rapidly along every path we took. At one point I heard voices. I stopped to listen. The voices came from the other side of the hedges. I stealthily peeked through the branches. I could see no one.

"Take a bit off the top there, boy." The man's voice was faint. "No, over to your left."

I kept my ear open as I continued my way to the center. The voice grew distant. It must be the same two gardeners I saw earlier. I hurried on. Before entering the smaller circle, I peered inside. There was no one there. I dashed to the bench, sat on it. I waited a moment, I heard no voices or footsteps. I leaned over, dug a small hole. Plato investigated it. I pushed him away. I stuffed the letter in the hole, and then covered it over. I sat for a few moments more, petting the dog. The gardener's voice reached me. I stood, walked toward the voice. It came from the northern part of the maze. I ran out the southern entrance. I returned to my lookout. Plato sat next to me.

The tall hedges supported me as I leaned back and closed my eyes. I was tired. My mind turned to the morning's events. So much had happened! I took out my watch, It was just past ten, though it felt like it was much later. The weather was turning warm. A bee buzzed overhead. He would soon leave as there were no flowers in the maze. I closed my eyes. There was stillness. After a moment, both gardeners' voices drifted towards me. Then their footsteps seemed to come my way. They grew louder. I stood.

"You be quiet, Plato," I whispered.

"Grab your rake. We need to go over the paths in this section." It was the man's voice again, only this time it seemed much closer to me.

I walked toward the other end of the dead end. The raking began. Then it stopped.

"Boss?" The voice belonged to a younger man.

"Yes, what is it?"

"There's a hanky here."

Footsteps traveled away from me. "Looks like a lady's. Better take it in to the lost and found. Do it now."

"Yes sir."

Footsteps ran toward me, then away. Then silence. The other man's footsteps now came toward the center of the maze. I silently scrambled to return to my lookout post. Holding my breath, I parted the branches. I had a direct view of the bench. The gardener began to rake all around it. He looked around as he did so. I quickly stood away from the hedge. The rake hit something hard. Carefully I returned to my viewport. The gardener raked out the note from its burial place under the bench. He leaned over and picked it up. Without looking at it, he shoved it into his vest pocket. He then continued raking toward the northern entrance. This was my chance. I quickly dashed back through the other way. I kept running, the dog at my heels, until I knew I couldn't go any further, that I had reached the last dead end. Now I had no choice but to create my own exit out of the maze. I searched for a thin place in the bushes. I had to break a branch, but with effort I was able to squeeze myself through the hedge. Plato crawled under the bush.

"Why Lady Bennet, what are you up to?" It was Sir John who spoke.

"I-"

"Is this your dog?"

He stood waiting for me to speak. He had removed his coat. He held it slung over his left shoulder. In his right hand he held a small cigar. He was all patience.

"I had lost the dog. Well lost myself, really."

"You became desperate, so you worked your way out this way." From where he stood, he looked over the small area of destruction I had created to facilitate my escape from the maze. "My, you are a clever girl." He returned his regard back to me. "The trouble I have with you is that nothing about you is English. Except for your dog here."

Plato sniffed Sir John's hand.

"I cannot help-"

"Tut, tut, tut, say nothing, but listen. You are quite fond of talking, and of, shall we put it politely, of weaving tales. None of which I believe. Except, that whatever you are up to, you display courage. I like that." He took a drag on his cigar. "Tell me, are you a part of a gang of thieves? Are you a confidence operation? Extortion?"

"I've no idea what you propose, sir."

He laughed at me. "I propose that you stop whatever it is you're doing because I cannot think you are engaged in it for legal reasons."

I turned to walk away. He grabbed hold of my arm. Plato growled. He dropped my arm.

"One minute more, then I will allow you to leave."

I glared at him with all the indignity I could muster.

"I am willing to claim you as my long lost niece if you will work for me."

"I beg your pardon."

"There is nothing you need worry about, and all you need do is carry on as you have been. I don't know what your present circumstance brings to you, in way of reward. I am willing to pay you outright. Think on it."

"Are *you* a thief?"

He chuckled. "No. I am a businessman." He stomped his cigar out in the dirt of the path. He kneeled down to pet Plato. "I have a little problem that you can help me with."

"What sort of problem?"

"Never mind that. All you need know is that your job will be easy, lucrative and enjoyable, I should think. A wedding and balls and such, what else could a young lady wish for?"

"I will think about it."

"Give me your answer at dinner."

I nodded. Sir John then stood and stepped back to allow me room to cross in front of him.

I followed the curve of the maze's outer edge, and then headed back to the hotel lobby. As I neared the entrance point, I came face to face with Martin.

"Well, young lady, what do you think of Sir John's offer?"

"How do you-? Oh, you were on the other side, listening."

"The hedge is high but sound travels quite well through it. I suspect you know this?" Martin motioned with his hand toward the hotel. We kept our silence until we were securely in our suite. Miss Cameron sat on the chair near the window.

"I've learned much from the maze." I sat on the settee and then related everything I had been through that morning to the both of them, about the man who picked up the note, and Sir John's proposal.

"He needs legitimacy of some sort. I wonder if he's a fraud?" Miss Cameron asked.

"He is not." Martin spoke.

"How do you know?"

"You have seen me at work, Miss Cameron. You know I have sources."

"So you do. Do you know what business this Sir John Symington-Reed is involved in?"

"Manufacturing. The South has little in the way of manufacturing. He met Mr. Hawkins in New York last year. They want to purchase the cotton to take to Sir John's mills in Manchester."

"Why not take it to a mill up north?"

"Their desire is to keep it away from the North."

"I think I understand their scheme."

"The question becomes how can we take advantage of his offer to Lady Ellen?"

"She is to play the niece and lend credibility to Sir John, or is she to be a bit of panache?"

"Perhaps a little of both."

"Hmm, how do we use this to our advantage?"

"A distraction."

"What about Marini?" I asked.

"Her exact fate cannot be known," Martin said. "Does she wait? Do we? Does her father keep her with him? Or sends her to the market here in Baltimore?"

"The market?"

"The slave market. Down by the wharf." Miss Cameron sighed deeply. "However, it could be a private sale. What ever method or decision Warton makes, we must speak to Marini, soon. Such a talk, of course, can be dangerous."

"Not if I speak to her."

"How's that, Lady Ellen?" Miss Cameron said. "After she heard the conversation between her mistress and Mr. Ewell, she is frightened out of her wits. How can you calm her, convince her?"

"I have a plan."

"What plan?"

"Miss Cameron, you tell me, often, that the less one knows the better."

Miss Cameron sat in silence. Then she rose. She checked her watch. "Time for dinner." She crossed to the mirror. "Come, Lady Ellen, let's fix your hair which is all out of sorts."

Not only did Miss Cameron fix my hair, she decided I needed to dress well for this important dinner where lies upon lies would be laid thick and fast. All in the name of rescuing a young lady who we were not certain wanted rescuing. Though her circumstances had changed, we could not be certain she still wanted to risk the trek from Baltimore to Philadelphia. Her situation could go from bad to worse if caught. With Gannon around, Vigilis might not save her even if he could. As for the others that would travel with Mrs. Tubman, would they want the kind of trouble that would come with Marini?

The pressure on me began to build. Martin suggested I take Sir John up on his offer, thus giving us a way to distract the Wartons.

Miss Cameron outdid herself with my hair and dress. My appearance was praised by those gathered for our dinner. Edward, Lavinia, Mr. Warton, Sir John, and Mr. Hawkins, each would agree I looked especially nice. Sir John sat next to me. He poured me a large glass of lemonade from the pitcher on our table. Miss Cameron was pleased. Truly pleased. Martin sat in the bar. The mirror over the bar allowed him to see us without turning around.

We finished our first course. Baltimore, known for its seafood, afforded us a delicious main course of crab.

"Have you had a chance to think over my little proposal?" Sir John whispered in my ear.

"I have."

"Lovely."

"I have a question, Sir John. How long should this ruse go on for?"

"What was that?" Mr. Warton asked.

"I asked Lady Bennet if she was joining us at Split Oaks." Sir John winked at me.

"Ah, yes, have you heard from your aunt?"

"Not as yet, " Miss Cameron said. "Though I expect to hear any minute now."

"The ruse could go on as long as you need it to," Sir John whispered to me.

Sir John, like Martin and Miss Cameron, was a good player at this game. I was improving. I don't know if the old me would have enjoyed it as much as the new me did.

"Oh," I said in an audible whisper.

"Is something wrong?" Lavinia asked.

"Please excuse me for a brief moment." I stood up. The men all stood and Sir John pulled the chair back for me.

"Can I help?" Miss Cameron said.

"No. I can find my way." I walked through the lobby to the lady's room. Now, I had a problem. I needed to speak to Martin, but could not go into the bar for two reasons. First, I would have to cross the opening of the dining room where I would be seen. Secondly, girls were not allowed in bars. I searched my purse to see if I had any dimes. I did. I then left the ladies' room, walked to the concierge and asked him for a piece of notepaper and a stylus or pencil. He pointed to a small desk nearby. I then wrote a note to Martin, telling him to come in to our meal with a telegram from my aunt giving me permission to attend Lavinia's wedding. The telegram was to have an addendum; that Sir John Symington-Reed was her cousin. I called for a bellboy, gave him the note and a dime, and instructed him to deliver the note to the butler, Botlieb, who was sitting in the bar.

"Wait," I then told the bellboy, "until I am seated at the table for five minutes before delivering this note."

"Yes miss." The bellboy then stepped away to point to the clock over the front desk. "At precisely one o'clock and sixteen minutes I will deliver this note to your butler. That gives you one minute to get to your table, and five minutes after, the note will be delivered. Satisfactory, miss?"

"Very satisfactory." I then marched off to the dining room.

Right on schedule, I watched as the bellboy delivered the note to Martin. Now it was up to him to create the rest of the grand drama we were acting in. From the corner of my eye, I saw Martin pay his bar bill, and then walk out into the lobby. It wouldn't be long now.

Inside, my heart raced but it was a different sort of racing. This time I looked forward to the next act in our play. Unlike an actor in the theater, I didn't know what was next, exactly. Would Martin take up my cue, or would he come up with an entirely different scenario for us to act out? What ever it was, the three of us, like the Musketeers of Dumas' novels, were one for all and all for one.

"Well?" Sir John whispered. He grew impatient.

I smiled. "What's for dessert?"

Chapter Nine

The Telegram

A fine piece of vanilla cake was placed before me. It nestled invitingly on a delicate plate of intertwining blue flowers on a white background. The silver fork seemed more polished than usual. The lemonade that poured from the crystal pitcher into my crystal goblet urged me to drink. It quenched the thirst stirred up by the nervousness of waiting for Martin to deliver the telegram. I wiped my mouth with the starched, white napkin. The corner was embroidered with the initials of the hotel. The LB stood out in the bright blue threads. Funny how I had not noticed it before. I picked up the fork.

Sir John leaned in toward me. He would whisper in my ear, to ask me again, what my decision was. I leaned away from him, as if to speak to Miss Cameron. And then someone cleared their throat.

"Lady Bennet?" Martin spoke. "This telegram arrived for you." He held it out to me on a silver plate.

"Thank you, Botlieb," I said as I took the telegram. Also on the plate was a small knife with which to open the seal. With all the grace I could muster, I broke the seal, returned the knife to the plate, and then straightened the paper. "Excuse me."

"Is it from your aunt?" Mr. Warton smiled as he spoke. "We all wait with baited breath."

I nodded my head. "Oh, it's lovely. She has given me permission to travel to Split Oaks."

"I'm so happy," Lavinia said as she clasped her hands in front of her. She smiled broadly to all of us.

"There is more," I continued. I turned to Sir John. "She says, Sir John, that you are a relation to me through my mother. My Mother was a Reed."

"She is one of the Derby Reeds, then, whilst I am one of the Yorkshire Reeds." Sir John said. He positively beamed. "Our paths, betwixt your mother and me, must have crossed before the falling out. It's regrettable, but these things do happen."

"Oh do tell, Sir John," Lavinia said. "If it is not too impertinent to ask."

"I know nothing of it," I said. I wanted to hear the story Sir John would make up.

"I am afraid it was one of those things that really was much ado about nothing. Sad, really, that the fuss over a piece of jewelry, that held very little monetary value, held so much sentimental worth that it forced a break between the Derby Reeds and the Yorkshire Reeds. When my grandmother, Lady Ellen Reed," Sir John turned towards me, "you know her as your great aunt," he turned back to the table, "when she died, her broken garnet necklace became a monstrous bone of contention. Who should have it?"

"Lady Ellen Reed? Were you named after her, Lady Bennet?" Lavinia asked.

"I believe I was."

"Yes, you must be," Sir John continued his story. "Your grandmother was heart broken. It was she that insisted your mother name you after her dear sister so that the connexion would not be lost. Or so this is what my sister told me."

Mr. Warton gave a "Humph."

"I have seen it, Sir John, a family torn asunder over nothing," Edward said.

"And what of the necklace? Who ended up with it?" Lavinia said.

"I did."

"You did?"

"Yes, Miss Lavinia. Granddad was so put out with the fighting that he took the piece and tossed it to me. "It's yours now!' he yelled out. That quieted the squabble between the cousins who were fighting over it. Cousin Elisabeth, your mother-"

"My mother?"

"Indeed. And Cousin Hannah, never spoke to one another again."

"That part, about the fight, that distresses me, though the story fascinates. I know so little of my family's history, thank you, Cousin John, I may call you cousin?" I said.

Sir John patted my hand lightly. "Indeed you may."

"What happened to Cousin Hannah?"

"Yes, tell us," Miss Cameron said. She too enjoyed the story and the performance that went with it.

"She married a gentleman from Brighton. I regret to inform you she died young, from complications during childbirth."

A strange feeling of sadness welled up inside me. It was as though I had known Cousin Hannah and now was sorry to lose her. "When did she die?"

"It has been twelve years." Sir John sighed deeply. He was sad as well. That sadness intrigued me. Did he act the part? Or was he truly sad?

"I'm afraid I was very selfish about the necklace. When Hannah was buried, she wore it."

This twist in the plot and the tone of his voice betrayed him. Sir John no longer made up a story. Someone in his past, someone he had loved, was gone from him. And he mourned her. After all this time had passed, he still felt the sorrow.

"I'm glad you gave it to her." It was now my turn to pat Sir John's hand.

"We shall make amends for the bad behavior of our respective family members." Sir John raised his goblet of wine. "Drink with me on finding my long lost cousin, Lady Ellen Bennet."

I was toasted and Sir John and I were congratulated. Our party grew merrier. With the removal of the dessert plates, the waiters now placed chocolates and other sweets on the table.

The grownups sipped brandy and port. Miss Cameron ordered a delicate tea for herself and me. She too enjoyed the party, but when the clock in the lobby struck the four o'clock hour, Miss Cameron stood up.

"It is past time for Lady Bennet's nap."

"Still napping, eh?" said Mr. Warton.

"Why Mr. Warton, young ladies must have their afternoon beauty rest. Surely you agree?"

"Why yes, Miss Cameron. It was said in jest."

"We must pack as well."

"Oh, you are quite right, Miss Cameron." Lavinia stood. "You gentlemen may finish your brandy, but I must see to the packing as well." Lavinia came around to where I stood. "I cannot leave it up to Maria to get it right. Someone must supervise her. I am so pleased you are coming to Split Oaks."

Arm-in-arm, we walked out of the dining room as Gannon walked it. Lavinia stiffened. "What are you doing here?"

"Good afternoon, Miss Lavinia. I see you know the young lady from Philadelphia."

"New York."

"Passing through Philadelphia was she? Odd that she should pass through *where* she did."

Miss Cameron came to my side. She took my other arm. "What business do you have with Lady Bennet?"

"Lady Bennet?" Gannon scoffed.

"What are you driving at, Gannon?" Mr. Warton approached us.

"'Tis this, Mr. Warton. This youngster you call Lady Ellen Bennet, why I saw her in Coonsville in Philadelphia. There she was, standing in the middle of the street. She wasn't dressed so fine as she is now, but it is the same girl, fancied up."

Lavinia gripped my arm tightly. "Liar," she said in a hoarse whisper.

"Edward," Mr. Warton called back to the table. "Take Lavinia to her room. Lady Bennet, please excuse us."

"Look here, man, what is it you're telling us?" Sir John spoke as he approached Gannon.

No one was leaving the dining room. Not Lavinia or Edward or Miss Cameron or me. Gannon looked around at the group and smiled his wicked smile. He was there to make trouble, and he had the audience he wanted in front of him.

"You can ask Vigilis. He saw her there as well."

"It is no business of yours where Lady Bennet goes." Miss Cameron started to lead me away.

"That is so. Except she was seen with the known abolitionist, Seth Peterson. And there's more, Mr. Warton. Vigilis thinks she knows where Lamentations is. That he is hiding in Philadelphia."

At this, Mr. Warton came around to me. "I want to think this is an absurdity." He looked at me, scrutinized my face, tried to read any emotions I may have displayed. "Is it?"

"Quite."

He looked me squarely in the eyes. I could see an idea flash through them. Quickly, he made up his mind.

"I apologize, Lady Bennet." He said it softly. He didn't want anyone else to hear him, only me. "This Lamentations is a most valued piece of property. I will pay handsomely for his return. Or for information as to his whereabouts. Anyone may collect the reward. Anyone."

"Mr. Warton, sir,I don't wish us to be a part of this scene," Edward said. "Come Lavinia." He led his fiancé out of the dining room.

"I am sorry, Mr. Warton, but I have no idea who this Lamentations is." I was becoming an adept liar. In a world as corrupt as the one these folks inhabited, it was my only choice. Miss Cameron squeezed my hand ever so slightly.

"Come, Lady Bennet. We need to be about our business." Miss Cameron firmly led me away.

In our suite, Martin had taken our bags out of the closet. "I heard the confrontation," he said as we closed the door. "We have little time now. Pack your things as if to leave with the Wartons in the morning. Keep out light clothing to wear."

A knock came. Miss Cameron stiffened.

"It's the bell boy, with the hot water." Martin crossed to the door. "We shall bathe while we have the chance to."

Three bell boys entered, each carrying two buckets of hot water. These they carried into the bathroom. Half the buckets were poured into the tub, the others were left on the side. Martin tipped them as they left..

"We will wash our hair as well," Miss Cameron said as she led me to the bathroom.

I dipped my hand into the water. "Too hot."

There was only the one faucet in those bathrooms. It was for cold water. Though this bath room was much better than the ones I had experienced in the eighteenth century, indoor plumbing still had a long way to go. I cooled the bath water down just enough to stand it. Miss Cameron then quickly and rather roughly washed my hair.

It felt good for I had not had a bath since Philadelphia. I wasn't used to being dirty except for my time as a soldier in the Continental Army. There I wore a uniform. Here, all the pretty clothing I wore meant I wanted to bathe more often.

When I was clean, Miss Cameron stepped into the tub. I washed her hair and then scrubbed her back. When we had finished, we turned the room over to Martin. We dressed simply in our shifts while our hair dried. Miss Cameron then braided our hair, allowing the braids to hang loosely down our backs. As the sun set, we dressed. We wore simple, dark colored skirts with blouses. As darkness settled over the room, the three of us sat in the parlor to eat a simple meal of bread, cheese and fruit. Miss Cameron stuffed more bread and cheese, along with jerky and nuts in a cloth bag. Martin took the bag when she was finished. This he placed alongside two jugs of water that sat next to the back window that looked out over the garden.

"At midnight, we will leave, through this window."

"Where are we going?" I asked.

"Back to Philadelphia."

"On the train?"

"No, Ell, not on the train. Gannon will watch the trains. Tonight, we must disappear into the darkness."

"But how then?"

"You ask too many questions, Lady Ellen." Miss Cameron smiled. "Whatever Botlieb has planned, you must obey him." She looked to Martin, but spoke to me. "We play a dangerous game, young lady. If you are caught, you could be arrested, and put into prison if they wish to make an example of you. I most definitely would be put in prison, and it would be far worse for Botlieb." Miss Cameron faced me and smiled.

"We shall sleep until eleven-thirty," Martin said as he took out his watch. "Now, to your rooms."

At precisely eleven-thirty, I was awakened. We gathered a few things to take with us, wrapping them in small throws. We had to travel light. I carried the bag of food so that Martin could carry the jugs filled with water.

We wrapped blankets around Plato for he too must be put to use. As we were prepared to exit out the back window, there was a soft knock on the door. We stood perfectly still. I held Plato's mouth shut. Martin put his finger to his lip. He walked quietly to the door. The knock repeated. Ever so gently he opened the door just a crack. He then reached out and pulled in Marini.

Martin sent Miss Cameron down first. He used a strong hemp rope, one end fashioned as a halter so that our descent would be easy and safe. The other end was wound around the side board which he had placed against the wall next to the window. He guided the rope, feeding out a little at a time until we reached the bottom. I was next, followed by Marini, and then came Plato. When he was out of the halter, I led Marini to the maze where we waited for Martin and Miss Cameron to fetch us.

From the maze, we walked out onto the hotel's back road where the delivery wagons traversed during the early morning hours. Away from the view of the hotel one such wagon waited. It was pulled by two dark horses. When we approached the wagon, Martin knocked on the sides. From the trees alongside the road, a man walked out. Without a word, he crossed the road to the wagon. He held out his hand to me. I took it and was helped into the wagon bed. Plato jumped in after me. When we were all in the wagon, the driver threw several light bags of cotton over us, then covered that with a tarp.

"No talking," he said.

We heard his footsteps walk to the front. He climbed up, sat down in the seat. The wagon lurched forward. Aside from the horses' hooves, for the next hour, we heard nothing save the occasional dog barking or an owl hooting. Plato wanted to bark back, but I kept my hand over his mouth.

How long this ride took I could not tell. I drifted in and out of sleep. When it finally stopped, I waited to hear the driver jump down but he didn't. Instead footsteps came from another direction. Soon the tarp was lifted at the back of the wagon. Martin was first to climb out. He, and Lamentations, helped the rest of us down. No one spoke. Lamentations led us to the shadows of the trees where Mrs. Tubman stood in the back of this small group of a dozen individuals, all waiting to walk to their freedom. The wagon driver slapped the reins across the horses back and then disappeared into the night.

Mrs. Tubman motioned for us to keep silent. For hours we followed her down a trail that led us through a woods that skirted a meadow. As the group passed it, we found ourselves in a deep woods that covered us in a protective night shadow. When the darkness before the dawn was on us, Mrs. Tubman pointed to her right by extending her arm out. She directed us into a small, enclosed area that was surrounded by heavy brush. When the last person had filed in, Mrs. Tubman followed. She then motioned for us to get close to her.

"We spend the day here. Sleep. Sleep close together so if you must say something to someone you can whisper in the ear. Nod your head if you understand this rule."

We all nodded our heads.

"Botlieb, Miss Cameron, come close."

I went with them even though she had not called my name.

"Miss Cameron, when I read Botlieb's note about that Gannon recognizing Ell, I knew he would watch the trains and coach depots. When he finds Marini and you gone, he will know he was right. It's nearly morning. As soon as he finds you are gone he will hit the road with a vengeance to find you. This is certain. In a few days we can put you on a coach. Botlieb tells me he and Ell have another way of avoiding Gannon."

"I'll be fine, Mrs. Tubman." Miss Cameron looked to Martin and me. "Fine."

The three of us found a small spot near Marini and Lamentations. Here we threw down our blankets and lay down for our first day of sleep. Plato curled up next to me. I recall the sun rising but I was so tired I turned my head away and fell back to sleep. It was later in the early afternoon when I woke. Plato was not near me. I got up to look for him. Walking through our camp I saw Mrs. Tubman resting, her back against a tree. In her hands she held a piece of bread which she picked at, taking small morsels into her mouth. Lamentations fussed over Marini. Miss Cameron helped a woman with a child prepare food for him. Martin leaned against a tree, his one leg bent, the other stretched out in front of him. He looked out toward the path. No one spoke unless they had to. Even the child sensed the gravity of his situation and kept his silence.

"Have you seen Plato?" I asked Martin in a whisper.

Martin pointed towards the woods. He then gave me food along with a cup of water. I knew I shouldn't eat too much as the food must last for how long, we could not know. With the edge off my hunger, I went in search of Plato. He was no where near the camp. I sat against a tree on the edge of the camp. From my sack I pulled out a small journal and pencil I had purchased at the hotel. It was here that I began to keep a diary.

After I filled a page with my thoughts of the last 24 hours, Miss Cameron came to me, brush in hand. She was determined that I should keep to the part of a young lady of the Victorian era. My hair was brushed and then braided. I was glad she groomed me because the act made me feel refreshed. Perhaps that is why human beings learned to groom themselves, because of what it did for the soul.

I sat with Marini and Lamentations for the rest of the afternoon. We whispered among ourselves.

"I wonder where we are," Marini said.

"We are about 15 miles outside of Baltimore," Lamentations guessed. "Tonight, we'll go further. Another 20 miles."

Plato came out of the woods. In his mouth he held a dead duck. This he dropped at my feet.

"What a good dog you got there, Miss Ell," Lamentations said. He picked up the bird and immediately begin to remove its feathers. "We will have a bit of duck for our super."

The remainder of the afternoon was spent in baking the duck on a bed of covered coals. Many folks praised Plato.

"He will be of use," Martin said. "Tomorrow, I shall take him out to search for more birds."

With the setting sun, Mrs. Tubman had us break camp. We drank water and met the calls of nature. Before the moon came out, we had returned to the path and headed in a northwest direction. We traveled in silence for hours. The boredom of it began to weigh heavily upon me. But the silence and the darkness were essential to our safety. Once we passed a farmhouse traveling way around its yard lest we wake the dogs. Plato was kept near so that I could silence his bark if need be. Perhaps sensing the necessity for silence, he kept it. Not one bark or growl escaped him all that night.

We walked through a field of corn, stealthily crossed a main road, and then waded through a pond, which gave way to a stream that flowed down from the north. Mrs. Tubman led us up this stream for at least an hour. By this trek through water our smell trail would be disrupted. Though a good tracker would guess we had taken a water route, it would take time to pick up our scent.

We came to a small waterfall. Here we stepped out of the stream and then went up a rather steep embankment to find ourselves by another pond. Here we rested.

After too short of a time, Mrs. Tubman roused us. We went up a small hill, and then down the other side, where we walked into a grove of trees. The child woke and grew fussy. His mother tried to calm him but he only wailed louder.

"Is he hungry?" Mrs. Tubman asked.

"I guess that be so," his mother said.

"We will rest here for a spell so that child can be fed."

We all sat down in a circle happy to be off our feet. The mother sat next to me. She gave the boy the nipple. He eagerly sucked .

"I guess this strange way of being makes him hungry at odd hours." The mother smiled weakly at me.

"How old is he?" I asked in the whisper we had all gotten used to using during our short conversations.

"He's just over two. I had him weaned when the other came along." The mother looked off into the black distance of the moonless night.

"The other one?"

"Yes, another boy." Her voice broke. "He died two weeks ago. That's when I decided."

"Decided?"

"That I would head north. That I would take the child left to freedom. Or die tryin'. Better to die tryin' I says to myself, then have another child that will die 'cause the master work me like a beast."

"What happened to the boy that died?"

"Neglect. That was it."

I could not see her face well, but I could hear the sorrow in her voice. She wanted to cry, but would not allow it.

"I was too far away from the cabin. There was no one to help me with that child, so he just up and died of neglect. Master, he swore at me, accused me of causin' the boy's death. Said I ruined his property."

Her resolve broke. She cried. "*His* property?" She lightly sobbed. "My child, from the day of his birth belonged to someone else."

The mother bent down and cried into her son's small chest.

"Her master was on a breeding program." Mrs. Tubman had sat next to us. "Wanted the women to have baby after baby. Exeptin' he did not give them extra time to care for 'em. These mothers was to go on like nothin' had changed for 'em. No wonder they died, babies and mothers too."

"Mrs. Tubman, I-" I shut my mouth because I was about to tell her that slavery would end in ten more years. But that would mean breaking one of the rules of time travel. I had already broken too many rules.

"Yes, Ell? What is it?"

Instead I said, "I believe, with all my heart, slavery will end."

"I want to believe that too. But sometimes my regard for the white man is so low that I lose all hope that they will do the right thing."

"They will, Mrs. Tubman. They will do the right thing."

Martin cleared his throat. He knew I wanted to cross the line to ease their pain. I silenced myself from saying anything further. The child had fallen back to sleep, so it was time to trek further north.

"In two days, I will ask you to leave the group."

"As you wish, Mrs. Tubman," Martin said.

"Having three whites is too noticeable in the dark. Not to mention the troubles you will have if caught."

"We promised to follow your orders, Mrs. Tubman."

"I will guide you to the Widow's Tavern, where the coach for Philadelphia stops." Mrs. Tubman counted heads. "We are all assembled." She turned to the west and stepped out into the night. We came to a road which we quickly crossed. On the other side, we entered another small forest. It seemed to grow darker. I looked up to see storm clouds gathering. In another thirty minutes, a downpour began. We each found a tree to somewhat shelter us. In another thirty minutes the storm moved southeast. Now we had to contend with a muddy path through the trees. All I could think of was how I wanted to lie down in a soft bed.

It grew colder as we marched northeast. Then we came to another small path that led along a farmer's back fence. I could make out cows sleeping on the ground not too far away. We followed this path that led us north through fallow cotton fields, and then picked wheat fields. From a small hill we could see a town off to the right. There was one light on in a house in the center of the town. Mrs. Tubman led us away from the town lest we be seen by whoever was up. The path then wrapped around a storage shed. Once on the other side, I could see the dawn breaking behind me. At a fork in the path, we headed west, toward trees. We crossed a brook, more, cold wet feet, and then entered another small forest. The stream meandered until it emptied out into a pond where a damn had been built. Here we were to rest for the day. I felt cold. I placed my blanket over me. With Plato curled against my back, in exhaustion, I fell asleep.

The next night and day were the same. By the third day I longed for an escape from this drudgery. I complained to Martin that I thought I would go crazy.

"That is irony, Ell."

"What do you mean?"

"We are surrounded by people escaping their drudgery. Except in their drudgery, they had no choice. Choosing this road, to freedom, is their first act of liberty; to choose the path they will take. They will find, though, that freedom does not offer an escape from the daily cares of life. In order to live, we must work hard."

"Marini will have to work hard. Is that what she was afraid of?"

"I think she was afraid she would have no work at all. A black can always work in the south. But in the North, there is the fact of whether or not a black will be accepted. And given work."

What Martin was saying confused me, for it never crossed my mind that the Northerners would be so prejudiced. How naive I was.

We walked a few more feet in silence. Then I said, "Edward told Lavinia he didn't want Marini as her personal maid, because at Cotton Wood they don't mix the races. What did he mean?"

"That means Edward has some standards. Warton has none. He takes what he wants. He acts the gentleman, but he has no idea what it means to be honorable." Martin smiled at me. "You learn more than you bargained for, ja Ell?"

"Ja, Martin, but another question I have is why does Vigilis slave hunt with Gannon?"

"Gives him power."

"Power?"

"To be a slave hunter, as a slave, now he has the power over the lives of men and women, children and even babies. But his power is not real, for in his pocket, he carries a note from his father allowing him to travel freely, from slave states to free states. Do you ask it, Ell, why he does not stay in the free states? Is that really your question?"

"Maryland is his home, and all that he knows." Miss Cameron had joined us.

We had come to our next resting place.

"I don't understand this thing about power."

"Get some sleep, Ell," Miss Cameron said. "Another time you can continue this philosophical discussion."

I was happy to obey. As was the habit, Plato curled up to sleep beside me.

That night, after we ate our meagre supper, we gathered our belongings and headed out. After about an hour, storm clouds gathered above us. To the southeast of us, lightening could be seen in the distance. Mrs. Tubman picked up the pace. Nonetheless, the wind whipped up and the rain began. Lightening flashed close by, and the thunder roared. We bent our heads and traveled on. Minutes ticked by. The incessant rain increased. The bolts of lightening were so close our hairs stood on end. Still we moved forward. The mother held her child close. I took her sack to help lighten her load. The ground grew steadily worse until it turned into a glue like mire. Nonetheless, Mrs. Tubman kept us moving. Another close bolt streaked across the black sky. It illuminated a small group of buildings not too far ahead of us. Finally, Mrs. Tubman called a halt.

"Mr. Botlieb, I leave you here," Mrs. Tubman said. "There's the tavern I told you of." She pointed with her chin toward the group of buildings.

"Thank you Mrs. Tubman. God speed." Martin slipped coins into Mrs. Tubman's hands.

"I'm glad I met you," I said to Mrs. Tubman. She gently touched my cheek. Lightening flashed. She had a smile on her face.

"I pray you are right, Ell, that slavery will end soon." She turned away with the thunder's roar to lead her struggling band of intrepid former slaves further into their freedom.

The three of us veered to the right as Mrs. Tubman's group trudged straight ahead, away from the road.

Once at the tavern, we found shelter in the barn. Inside, Martin took out his watch. It read 5:43. It would be another hour before it was light. Martin clicked on the watch's stem. He was calling the time chair.

"The coach that will take you to Philadelphia arrives at ten o'clock."

"And you two?"

"We have a coach that will pick us up. For now, we will wait with you to see to it you are safely on yours."

"I appreciate that."

"I'm tired and hungry. Do you think we could get into the inn?" I peeked out the side door of the barn which faced the tavern. "There's a light on."

Martin looked the tavern over. "Someone is up. I would say the kitchen fire is being stoked. The cook prepares breakfast." He turned to me. "Shall we knock on the door and beg the cook's mercy?"

"I say yes." Miss Cameron pushed the door open all the way. She stepped out into the stable yard. Just then a huge flash of lightening filled the yard with light. Standing in the middle of the yard was Gannon. Miss Cameron gasped. Gannon smiled.

Chapter Ten

Complex Travel Arrangements

Plato ran out of the barn with a growl. He hated Gannon more than any human did.

"Plato! Come back!" I tried to follow him out, but Martin held me back.

Plato incessantly barked as he had done that night he had chased me through the woods outside of Trenton in 1777. Only the thunder could drown the noise. I could see the shadow of the dog as he bounced around Gannon looking for a way to get to the man's throat.

A bolt of lightening flashed across the scene. Gannon went for his gun.

"No!" I screamed.

Martin forcefully pulled me away from the door. "You stay here!" he shouted as he left the barn.

"Vigilis!" Gannon yelled out.

I went back to the door to watch the scene as it played out. The next flash of lightening revealed that Miss Cameron had grabbed hold of Plato by his collar. Gannon took advantage of the dog's control to run to the road in front of the tavern. I could no longer stay in the barn.

"Miss Cameron!" I grabbed hold of her, to force her to look at me. "He'll pick up their trail!"

We both ran around to the road as Vigilis ran out of the tavern. He headed for the barn. Martin followed him. Miss Cameron let Plato loose and he ran straight for

Gannon, and without hesitation, he jumped him. knocking him to the ground. I couldn't see the details of this man and dog fight, but my fear was that Gannon would kill my dog. I ran towards them fighting off Miss Cameron who attempted to stop me. When I reached them, I pulled Plato off. Gannon tried to go for his gun, but he didn't have it. It lay on the ground not more than four feet away.

"If you go for that gun, I will turn the dog loose!"

Miss Cameron ran for the gun. Gannon rolled over to crawl for it as he was closer to it than Miss Cameron. I was about to release Plato when I heard hoof steps behind me. It was Martin, atop a horse, coming towards us.

Martin jumped from the horse in front of Gannon. The two men now fought, fists to face and backs as Martin kept Gannon from reaching his gun. This gave Miss Cameron time to get to it. She picked it up. Just as she did, a third man came out of the tavern We had never seen him before. As Miss Cameron ran back toward the barn, he ran after her. As another streak of lightening stretch across the distant sky, this man shoved Miss Cameron to the ground.

I let Plato loose. He went towards this other man who used his male strength to grab the gun. This is when Vigilis came out, riding one horse and leading another. The man jumped on the second horse.

Martin threw Gannon to the ground, and he then jumped on the horse he had been riding. As the rain lessened, and the thunder and lightening moved south, Martin urged the horse into a full gallop as if to follow the storm. Horse and man flew down the road. Gannon struggled up, wiped the blood from his mouth. He looked to the third man.

"Give me the horse!"

The third man dismounted. I grabbed hold of the reins of Vigilis' horse.

"Let them go!" I yelled out.

"Can't do that!"

"Yes, you can." With my right hand, I grabbed hold of his leg. "You can!"

"Let me go!" He forced his horse forward.

"She's your sister!"

He turned back to me. "If I don't bring her back, my father won't free me."

So there we had it. Vigilis' true goal was himself. Not at all like Lamentations who risked it all to bring his sister into freedom. As the lightening lessened and the thunder was a distant sound, I found clarity.

"It's not Gannon! It's you!" I ran towards him but he turned his horse to face the road. "You would own slaves if you could!" Vigilis spurred his horse on. "You're worse than your father!" I called after him as he galloped away.

I tried to run after him, but the third man pulled a gun from his holster, fired a shot into the sky.

"Halt!" he cried out. "You are interfering with a lawful attempt to retrieve the property of George Warton!"

"Never!" Miss Cameron shouted. She hit the man's leg with a rock. "You're a beast!" She ran to him, hands out, reaching for his face. "A beast!

"Lady! Stop this!"

For a second time this man knocked Miss Cameron to the ground. I ran to her. Plato attacked him, his mouth closed firm around his ankle. He pulled the gun. I heard a loud bang. Fearing the worst, I turned around expecting to see my dear dog dead. Instead, a petite woman stood at the back door, a rifle in her hands. Plato was much alive and growling at the man.

"Whose dog is it?" the woman said.

"Mine."

"Call him off."

"Plato!" He obeyed. He sat quietly by my side.

"Ma'am," the man spoke. "My associates and I are here lawfully attempting to retrieve the property of George Warton of Maryland."

"Slavers, huh. I was suspicious about you when you showed up last night." The woman walked toward the man. "Caruthers, right, that's your name?"

"Yes, Mrs. Hunter."

"Who are you?" Mrs. Hunter asked Miss Cameron.

"I am Miss Cameron, this young lady's governess."

"And the young lady with the dog?"

"Lady Ellen Bennett."

"Lady?" Mrs. Hunter eyed me, and then Plato. "The dog seems well bred, so I guess I'll buy that, for now."

"Now Mrs. Hunter, please, I need to join my associates."

"Now Mr. Caruthers, you are in Pennsylvania."

"Doesn't matter. The law says we can retrieve our property without interference. In any state."

"But you may not have a brawl on my property!" Mrs. Hunter kept her rifle pointed to the ground, yet in

Caruthers direction. "Especially fighting a woman and a girl."

"There was a man in the fight, but he left them here to fend for themselves."

"I saw the thing from my window up there." Mrs. Hunter motioned with her head towards the third floor window. "Three grown men against one man, one dog, one girl and one woman. Doesn't seem like a fair fight to me, though between this dog and these two ladies, they almost had you licked." She chuckled. "I tell you what, Caruthers. You pay up for you and your associates, and then I'll let you hightail it out of here."

"How much?" Caruthers started to reach for his pocket.

"Stay out of there." Mrs. Hunter lifted her rifle up to point it at him.

Caruthers' hands became motionless.

"You, Lady Ellen, you reach into his pocket and retrieve six dollars."

"Six?" Caruthers was surprised. "We stayed only the one night."

"And ate three suppers, boarded three horses. If I had known you were slave hunters, I would have left you to the storm. Go ahead, young lady."

I walked over to Caruthers. He looked at me with hatred, but he was a patient man in control of his emotions. Plato walked close to me, stayed right at my side. Caruthers knew that if he attacked me or made a false move in anyway, Plato would lay into him. He also knew that the sooner he cooperated with Mrs. Hunter, the sooner he could be on his way.

"The money is in the side pocket inside my coat." He motioned with his eyes.

I reached in. Nestled in the pocket I could feel several coins. I pulled them out. They were silver dollars. I counted out six from the nine he had. I returned the three into his pocket. When I turned around to walk to Mrs. Hunter, I saw that there was a man with a shotgun standing in the front yard of the tavern. No wonder Caruthers had turned docile. I handed her the six coins. Without taking her right hand off the rifle, she took the coins in her left, and then counted them. These she placed in the pocket of her apron.

"Get on your horse now and leave. Don't ever come back this way."

"Ma'am, they took my horse."

"I guess you are walking." With her rifle, Mrs. Hunter motioned for the man to leave. He did. When he reached the road, he broke out into a run.

The rain had now completely stopped. The clouds turned pink with a rising sun breaking through them. The four of us watched as the man disappeared around the bend in the road. Only then did Mrs. Hunter put down her rifle.

"Who is the man with you?" Mrs. Hunter questioned Miss Cameron.

"Mr. Botlieb. He is Lady Ellen's butler."

"You an English lady?"

"Yes ma'am." The ruse was back on. "We were hounded by these men."

"Mmm." Mrs. Hunter was suspicious. "Bart!" The man who held the shotgun came toward the landlady.

"Saddle up. Ride after them. See what transpires and see if you can't get that English butler saved."

The man nodded then hurried to the stable.

"And what are you? English as well?" she asked Miss Cameron.

"American."

"What I have here is a young English girl, her American governess, her butler run off, and a hunting dog traveling together, on foot. Doesn't sound very lady like to me." She looked us over. We were a sorry lot, wet, muddied, totally disheveled. "You look tired and hungry. Got any money?"

"Yes." Miss Cameron produced her purse.

"Breakfast is on. Follow me."

"I'm worried about Botlieb," I said to Mrs. Hunter.

"Dear one, he looks like a man who can take care of himself." Bart rode off down the road. "Bart is a good shot. Though I suspect your man Botlieb is leading them *away* from someone. You don't have to answer that." She smiled at me. "We'll include the dog in the meal price."

In the worst way I wanted to look up to the hills, to know that Lamentations and Marini and the rest had gotten far away. That, however, would be a mistake. It wasn't only talk that could lead to their capture. A look in the right direction could as well. The slavers were savvy and they watched like hawks for signs that someone knew something. It hadn't taken Gannon long to figure out that I knew something. So I fought off the impulse to gaze. No one would learn anything from me.

The dispersing clouds widened their gaps. The sun was now up. Mrs. Tubman would be settling down her group of intrepid fugitive slaves. They would soon be asleep. My stomach growled. I was the fortunate one. I would soon have a large breakfast of ham, eggs and biscuits. What would that mother have? Or Lamentations? Or Marini? Or the rest of the dozen slaves that traveled the road to freedom.

"Come, Lady Ellen, let's go inside." Miss Cameron took my arm and led me into the tavern.

The landlady led us to a washroom attached to the tavern's mudroom. "Towels and soap are two bits each. The water service is a dollar for both of you if you'd like a bath."

Miss Cameron reached into her miser's purse to remove the coins.

"I can get the laundress to wash your clothing if you have nothing clean to wear." Mrs. Hunter waved to a young boy who washed dishes. "We're having a bath here, Tommy."

Tommy left off washing to grab buckets for the water.

"We have clean underwear. Only the skirts and blouses need attention." Miss Cameron opened her purse again. "How much?"

"Pay Maggie directly." Mrs. Hunter walked over to the stairs. "Maggie! Customers!" she shouted up. She returned to where we stood. "She's also the maid around here. Can't run the place without her."

Maggie, a woman of about 35, ran down the stairs. She looked over our clothes." Where you been?"

"They got caught up in the storm, Maggie. Can't you see that?" Mrs. Hunter winked at us.

"Oh yes, Sarah, I see what you mean. I can have them ready for you in three hours. For a dollar."

Miss Cameron pulled out the last coin in her purse to hand to Maggie. Mrs. Hunter sat us down at the table in the kitchen. We were not fit to eat in the dining room. She made us fried eggs, ham, grits and gave us leftover biscuits. She did not charge us for the biscuits. By the time we had eaten, and Miss Cameron worked on her third cup of coffee, Tommy came in to announce the bath was ready. Mrs. Hunter had set up everything, so all we had to do was take our baths. Maggie came in to help us undress and took our muddied, torn and filthy clothing. We scrubbed ourselves down.

"I am worried about Botlieb."

"It's been nearly an hour." Miss Cameron poked her head out the small window that faced the stables. "I can see the road a bit. I don't see anyone on it. Not even Mrs. Hunter's man, what was his name?"

"Bart."

She returned to combing her wet hair. "I wonder if the coach will arrive on time?"

"I don't even know the time." I kept to the bath a while longer. The water was still warm, and so relaxing.

Plato barked. Miss Cameron looked out the window.

"There's someone now." She stretched her neck out to get a better view. Seeing something, she turned back to me. "Get out. It's that man, Bart. He's back."

"We still have no clothes."

"We have our fresh shifts." Miss Cameron poked around in one of our bundles. "And here's my shawl. Perhaps Sarah can supply another shawl or blanket."

There was a knock on the door. I wrapped the towel around me. A voice called out from the other side. "It's Sarah. My man has returned with some news about your butler."

Miss Cameron opened the door. She stood in her shift with her shawl wrapped around her. Mrs. Hunter gave us both a look, and then turned around. "Maggie, bring me a sheet." Maggie took one out of her laundry basket. She handed it to Miss Cameron. "You wrap up in this and give the shawl to the girl." She closed the door.

Miss Cameron wrapped the sheet around her, turning it into an attractive Greek like gown. She looked like a Greek goddess. Once I had my shift on, the shawl was wrapped around me in a shorter version of the goddess outfit. We then walked out in our bare feet. We were too anxious to learn what the man had to say to care about shoes or even stockings. Everyone gathered in the kitchen. While Maggie ironed, we sat around the kitchen table. Bart came through the mudroom, removed his boots before he proceeded in.

"Well?" Sarah said.

The man's face and body were splattered with mud. Maggie handed him a wet cloth. He wiped his face.

"This has been the strangest day of my life."

"How so?"

"After I took off down the road, I passed that Caruthers, who was just walking at that point. He looked all around himself, figuring to find Gannon, I suppose. As I near Old Wiley's corn field, I see that black kid at a gallop, riding hard away from the back woods there. It's a good thing old Wiley didn't see him."

"Never mind that. Tell us what happened."

"I keep pressing Bones ahead, and finally I caught sight of that Gannon character. But he isn't going after that butler. No ma'am. He is stopped dead in the middle of the road."

"Whereabouts?"

"Jus' the other side of Old Wiley's barn, where the road curves round it. I slowed down to see if the butler was near. I don't see him nowhere. Then, me and that Gannon, at the same time, both spot the horse the butler been riding. The horse is riderless. Gannon jumped off his horse. I kept to mine to see what's on the other side of the barn." Bart spoke directly to Miss Cameron. "I admit I was scared that I was going to see a body, but there was none. It was like that butler disappeared."

"What did Gannon do when he didn't see him?" Mrs. Hunter said.

"Well he jumped down from the horse he was riding to claim his own mount again. He got up on *his* horse jus' as the black boy comes out of the cornfields. He has a dumbfounded look spread across his face. 'What's a matter with you?' Gannon asks him. The boy jus shakes his head. Somethin' scared him good. I pull up. Gannon rides toward the boy. The boy said, 'Don't go in there!' Now you know as well as I that a man like Gannon has to got to go in."

The man tossed the wet cloth into the sink. Maggie had stopped her ironing to listen.

"And then?" Mrs. Hunter grew impatient.

"I rode around to the other side of the barn. I wanted to have a look inside, to see if that butler fellow was in there. I rode right in. I looked all around. Got off my horse, climbed up to the loft. No one was hiding up there. Then I hear yelling. I came back out to see the boy fly past me. He yelled out, 'I ain't goin' back in there!' I admit that my curiosity overcame any sense I may have. Just as I was about to enter the cornfield, a bright light flashed in front of me. Like lightening it was, but low to the ground. This was followed by a strange noise I have never heard before. My horse got unruly, no, he didn't like it neither. I didn't see Gannon about, but someone galloped off on the other side of the flashing light. I calmed my horse. I urged him forward. I wanted to know what had caused the light and what had made that sound. I went ahead about twenty paces and then I came to a place where the corn lay flat, in a square. Some of the other corn was leaning away from it, some burned a bit. It surprised me that the dried leaves hadn't turned the entire field into an inferno.

As the man spoke I knew exactly what he had come upon.

"And the butler?" Miss Cameron said.

"No where I could see, ma'am. I decided to ask Old Wiley if he knew anything. When I come out of the field, Gannon is talkin' to the boy and Caruthers is now sittin' on his horse. They have the same idea as me. Gannon rides up to Old Wiley's house. Old Wiley came out just as I rode up. 'What's that strange thing that goes on in your cornfield?' Gannon asks. 'It is a strange storm we had,' Old Wiley tells him. 'Jus' as the lightening stops, one hits the cornfield with an awful noise. I see the stalks shiver, some burst into flames, and then I heard a hiss. I stayed away as I don't want to get struck by any lightening.' "

I leaned back against the wall. At last, the Time Chair had arrived. It had Martin, of that I was certain. Where he would take it next I didn't know. I was confident he was coming back for me, and, hopefully, it would be today.

The dog barked again. We heard horses in the yard. Mrs. Hunter looked out the window.

"Gannon," she said as she grabbed her rifle. She marched to the back door, opened it, and then stuck out her rifle aimed at Gannon. "What do you want, Gannon?"

"I want to talk to the woman. Or the girl."

"No!"

"We can shoot it out if you want, Mrs. Hunter."

"You would dare that? And get yourself arrested? Is the property you're after worth that much?"

"The property is priceless." Gannon looked over the tavern. "There's enough money for all of us." Gannon pointed to Caruthers. He moved toward the southern part of the tavern. "But there's more. Ask that little girl where she is really from?"

"Her money is good. That's all I care about. I am tavern keeper, not a gossip. As for your proposition, I don't much like slavery."

Gannon laughed from his throat. "I don't much care for it either. Having felt the whip myself. I am Irish, Mrs. Hunter, a hater of the English. They took me when I was a boy, younger than that girl in there. I was sent to Jamaica to toil in their fields. I tried to run, twice. First time out, they just whipped me. Second time out they killed the priest who had helped me. That time, hope died in me. That is when I became the meanest bastard among all the poor red legged, mean bastards who worked themselves to their early grave. Warton, who had come to our plantation to find Irishmen who wanted to become foremen on his plantation, bought me. You see now, don't you, just like that little nigger who runs with me, I am owned by Warton as well. Not legally. But in here," he pointed to his heart. "I owe the man for getting me out of that hell." Gannon spit on the ground. "Now that girl you have in there is not English. No ma'am. She is as American as you are."

Mrs. Hunter looked my way. She scrutinized my face. She turned her gaze to Miss Cameron. "Well, what about it?"

"She is Lady Ellen Bennet, born in Derby."

Mrs. Hunter smiled a slight smile. "I bet that's all you know, isn't it." She turned to Maggie. "Get their clothes ready. The coach to Philadelphia will be by in an hour." She turned back to Miss Cameron. "The coach. That is what you're here for?"

Miss Cameron nodded. Mrs. Hunter poked her head back out the door. "They are leaving on the ten o'clock coach. Why don't you ride up the road a ways to have a talk with them there."

Gannon thought about it. He looked to Caruthers, then pointed with his chin up the lane. Caruthers trotted off. Gannon dismounted his horse and sat on rock in the shade by the road. Vigilis was no where to be seen.

Maggie finished our clothes. I paid her the money. In the washroom, we dressed.

"I don't know what's to happen to us, Lady Ellen. Without Botlieb to watch over us, circumstances might become problematic." She sighed, deeply.

"Miss Cameron, you are the victim of certain, shall I say, mishaps on my part."

"Oh dear, please do not tell me any more."

"It is necessary." I slipped back into my American accent. "It has nothing to do with the whereabouts of a group of people we know of. It has to do with whom I really am. Gannon is right. But you know that I am an American girl. What you don't know is about the journey I am on. This journey, however, is, oh how shall I put this. It's a mistake. Botlieb was sent to find me. Once he found me, he helped me do what I had set out to do. He protected me, you, even the dog." I took Miss Cameron's hands in mine. "He continues to do so." Just then my watch began to chime. I reached into my purse and pulled it out. I clicked it open. The little light was blinking rapidly. The time chair was near. "I have to go. But when you get on that coach, we will be nearby."

I made for the door, but Miss Cameron grabbed my skirt. "Wait! You and Botlieb will be nearby? How do you know this?"

"I can't tell you." I ran out the door and into the yard. Plato ran up to me. The watch indicated the chair was to my left. That would be in the orchard bordering the stables. I ran toward it.

Miss Cameron followed me out. When she saw me head for the orchard, she walked quickly behind. I climbed the fence and then ran through the trees that were neatly lined up. The red light grew brighter.

"Ell!"It was the Old Man, standing in between two trees, dressed in a pair of old trousers, a linen shirt and a broad brimmed hat.

"Professor!" I ran to hug him.

Our greeting was stopped by a scream. Martin then came down the row. He ran towards the scream.

"Come, let's get to the chair, quick."

"But Martin?"

"Come along Ell. You too, Plato."

The Old Man pulled me through several rows of trees until we came to a thicket of shrubs. He parted the bushes. Inside was the Time Chair inviting me to its safety. No one had to tell me to make my seat.

"Stay there. Do not touch anything." The Old man retraced his steps.

The waiting seemed interminable. From my seat, nothing could be seen. Plato's ears picked up. Something had attracted his acute attention. Now I heard it too. Running footsteps accompanied by grunts. I could stand it no longer. Plato and I went back out into the orchard. There was Martin fighting with Gannon, and Miss Cameron trying to break a branch off a tree. The Old Man came round to her to break the branch for her. He then tried to take it from her, but she was so angry she grabbed it back. She marched over to where Gannon had Martin pinned against a tree. Gannon didn't see it coming. She hit him hard, twice. He was stunned. Martin grabbed Miss Cameron. The Old Man was already coming towards me. He nearly did a nose dive through the bushes. I turned to follow. The Old Man powered up the machine and it began its whine. Martin shoved Miss Cameron onto the seat, then picked me up and placed me on her lap. Martin squeezed in. I swung my legs over across the Old Man's lap. The glass was coming down when Gannon parted the bushes. But Plato side swiped him and then jumped onto the floor.

"Get back or you will be dead!" Martin shouted out.

Gannon stepped back. The fog readily curled up over the glass as it sealed tight. The whine sounded welcoming. I turned to smile at Miss Cameron, who had a rather wild look on her face. The machine whirled fast, the lights began their show. The blackness then enveloped us.

When I came to the glass was lifting up in the middle of the warehouse. Miss Cameron hugged me tightly, her face buried in my back. The Old Man shook his head so that he would come to faster. Plato ran out, while Martin did his best to follow him before the enclosure was all the way up. When the Chair's cycle was complete, Martin helped me out. He then held out his hand to Miss Cameron, who, unsteady on her feet, was introduced to the twentieth century.

She kept silent as she slowly looked around the large room. We gave her time. The Old Man headed for his office. Martin fiddled with the dials. Fatigue quickly settled over me.

"What is your name?" Miss Cameron asked, turning to me.

"Ell. Ell Evans. What's yours?"

"Mary Keaton. Spinster and abolitionist. And Botlieb?"

"Martin. Martin Botlieb.
"You mean that is your real name?" I said.

"So it tis."

"You intrigue me, Mr. Botlieb." Mary smiled ever so slightly.

"We must talk, at some later date." Martin went to the back of the Chair. "At this time, we must make amends for this young lady's mishap." He removed the clock in the back. "First, I will check this clock again."

"What happened to me?" I said.

"This clock malfunctioned. It should have taken you to 1854 as you set in the dials. That is why we always recheck the dials before we leave."

He lectured me.

"But how did Lamentations get here? Was that a malfunction?"

"Somehow, he tripped the mechanism. We are not sure how, but ja, it was not entirely your fault, Ell."

"What are you talking about? Where exactly am I?"

"In place where you cannot stay." The Old Man came out of his office carrying another clock. "Try this one. Take it on a maiden voyage before we return the lady to where she belongs." Martin placed the new clock in its place. "You, Miss Cameron, that is not your real name, is it?"

"I take on different names depending on the role I am to play."

"Underground railroad?"

"Yes,. Lady Ellen, that is, Ell, called you professor?"

"Clawson. Professor of physics, emeritus, Howard University." He gave a bow from the waist. "At your service."

"I don't know this university."

"Not yet. But you will." The Old Man smiled broadly at Mary. "You are one of the ones who will make it possible, in your own way. You are one of those unsung heroines, fighting the good fight without acknowledgement, without praise. For the abolitionist works for a greater glory, do you not?"

"I cannot imagine Judgment Day without the ability to tell my God that I struggled against evil. That is correct."

"And now, Miss Mary Keaton, you will go back and continue your struggle."

We turned toward the Chair when we heard the engine whine. The Old Man took my hand and then Mary's hand, to lead us to his office. When the door was shut, we heard the sounds that the chair was gone.

Mary took a seat by the desk. I ran into the bathroom to change back into my clothes. From the bathroom, I listened to the conversation.

"What does that contraption do? Will you at least tell me that?"

"How educated are you, Miss Keaton?"

"I read, write, understand math. I read philosophy with Miss Carston at her academy. Reverend Weber, though somewhat reluctantly, tutored me in the classics. I learnt Latin and Classical Greek."

"My. For a woman of the nineteenth century, your education is amazing. But then would you have thought a black man would be a professor?"

"A woman of the nineteenth century?" Mary fell silent. "What...I mean to ask...actually, I am rather frightened."

"Understandable."

A car honked its horn.

"What was that?" Mary asked.

"Would you like a glass of sherry? Or port. I've both."

I didn't hear a response. I heard the Old Man push his chair back. This was followed by footsteps. I then heard him call to me near the bathroom door.

"What about you, Ell? Is it allowed?"

I opened the door. "Should I show her how I am dressed?"

"That might soften it." He moved away to a cabinet under the high window.

I walked out. Mary's mouth fell open when she saw me dressed in my blue jeans and white cotton shirt.

"You wear trousers?"

I deduced that I should tell her. "Miss Keaton, Mary, it isn't 1854 anymore."

"What year is it?"

"1974."

The Old Man was there with the sherry right on time. He gave her the glass. She downed it. She held it out for more. She sipped that one. She licked her lips. We waited. We could see she was thinking. The Old Man understood, that with her education, her obvious intelligence, that she would figure out that some wondrous thing had happened to her.

"That contraption." She whispered. "It flies through the heavens in some way to take us to a different year." She looked to the Old Man. "Do I have the gist of it?"

"You do."

We could see her mind was working rapidly, putting things together. "You," she pointed to me, "you said something happened that wasn't supposed to."

"Yes."

"What happened?"

Before I could answer, we heard the chair returning. We kept silent until its noise died down completely.

"That will be Martin," the Old Man said. He returned to his seat behind his desk.

The door opened. Martin walked through wearing his butler clothing. "Ready."

"Miss Keaton, it is time for you to leave us."

"But I have so many questions?"

"I do apologize for the way we have inconvenienced you, and put you into danger. Ell didn't mean to do what she did. Did you Ell?"

I ran to Mary and put my arms around her. "I am so sorry. But I am not sorry, not sorry at all that I met you. I shall never forget you. Never. We made a good team, the three of us."

Mary held me close for a time. She then took my arms from her, kissed my forehead. "We made an excellent team." She followed Martin into the warehouse. I was sad to see her go.

"Now, young lady, you have some things to settle."

I nodded my head.

"What we must do is complex. That means you obey Martin every step of the way. We are uncertain if everything will work out, but try we must. Do you understand?"

"Yes sir."

"Martin will take you back to 1924. When you arrive, you will see yourself there, with this Lamentations and Plato. Listen carefully. It is extremely dangerous to encounter yourself when time traveling. So you must not, ever, try to speak or interact with your other self. Avoid it at all costs. Do you understand that?

"I will see me, as I was?"

"Yes. However, I need a confirmation from you that you will obey our instructions. To the letter."

"I will."

"Your one function while there is to stop that dog from crossing the street."

"I understand."

We heard the chair leaving. We waited for the silence before continuing our conversation.

"I understand the dog was shot by Gannon in 1854?"

"He was." I explained how we saved Plato.

"I should have sent that dog back when he came through, but I was in too much of a hurry to get to my grandmother's." He scowled. "Nonetheless, if someone should come through again, like Lamentations did, you need to send him and the chair back.

"Wouldn't he have ended up in 1924?"

"You have a point." He drummed his fingers on his desk. "If, and that is the big if, because Martin and I have taken measures, if that happens again just wait and send the chair back empty."

"How do I do that?"

"I didn't teach you how to use the watch?"

"Only a little. Come to think of it, professor, there is much you need to tell me."

"I see. When you return, you are to have lessons." He looked away. He was angry with himself.

"Professor."

"Yes."

"I'm hungry."

He went to the small kitchen. I heard him rifling around for a minute. He then returned with a plate of sandwiches and two Pepsis. He set this on the desk.

"Eat."

I gobbled up a turkey sandwich. The Pepsi tasted so good I thanked whatever god would listen to me for having been born in the twentieth century.

"Want some ice-cream?"

I nodded. He returned to the kitchen for the ice cream. Satisfied, I put my head on the desk, ready for a nap. The Chair announced its return. It was my turn. One more trip this day before my work was done. Even I knew this task could not be put off. Martin came in. Without a word I returned with him to the time chair.

"Is she alright?"

"She is."

I didn't ask anything more because I didn't want to know. Martin powered up the engine, the glass came down, the lights sparkled, and then the next thing I knew, we were in 1924. Martin had set the Chair down in a well hidden place near the Assunpink Creek. He helped me up the embankment. He took out his watch.

"In five minutes, you, Lamentations and Plato will arrive. Come, show me where the accident happened."

We walked to Broad Street. I pointed out where I saw the car after the accident, and where I had found Plato. Martin directed me to cross the street. In the shadow of a building we waited.

"Soon now, you will see Plato. Cross over and wait for him. Shoo him away, back toward the orchard."

As instructed, I crossed the street. Out of the darkness I saw the dog coming toward the street. Next came Lamentations running down the alley. Before Plato hit the sidewalk, I jumped in front of him.

"Plato, no!" That was my other self calling out.

"Get away!" I said, waving my arms to him. "Get away!" He turned to try and get around me. I dashed to the side to ward him off. For whatever reason, Plato wanted to cross that street. I kept running sideways. When I heard the car pass behind me, I stopped to see if that was the car that had the accident. It wasn't. Plato did an end run around me and then headed for the street. I heard the breaks and then the sound of the dog being hit. I could see myself coming towards me. I turned to run. But Harry Caruthers jumped out of his car to see if the dog was alive. I ran, dodging traffic from the other way. Martin stepped out of the shadows and grabbed me. We hid to watch the scene unfold to see if our scheme had worked. As we watched, my old self came out of the alley and stopped dead in her tracks when she saw Plato laying dead on the road.

"Sorry, miss, but he ran out right in front of me before I could stop," Harry Caruthers said. "Such a nice looking dog. What a shame."

As my old self listened, I saw Lamentations come out of the alley. Harry saw him as well.

"I just got him," my old self said.

"What do you want?" Harry said to Lamentations.

"Nothin'."

"He works for us."

"Pick up the dog there, boy."

Lamentations went to the dog and picked him up.

"Our job here is done," Martin said to me.

We started to walk back to the time chair, except an overwhelming vertigo came over me. I grabbed hold of Martin's arm. The spinning didn't stop.

"Ell? Ell?"

Martin's voice faded into a strange distance. I passed out.

I seemed to dream. In the dream, I was in 1854 again. Mrs. Bishop was there, as well as Marini, Lavinia, Miss Cameron and then Gannon. Plato barked. Someone picked me up to move me. There was shouting. My hands felt for whatever it was that kept me lying down. There was nothing solid beneath me. I seemed to float in the noise below me. I felt sick. Here I floated until the Old Man's voice filled my ears. "Ell? Ell?" I plunged into a cold bath. I shivered. Plato jumped in after me, licked my face. "Ell, Ell?" That was my mother's voice. "Ell, how do you feel now?" I didn't know that man's voice at all. The bath turned warm. Plato panted.

"Ell, how do you feel now?" the man's voice asked again.

"Grandpa?"

That was me who spoke. I opened my eyes to see my grandfather staring me in the face.

"Grandpa?"

"Ell? How do you feel now?"

"Grandpa!" I reached up to hug him with all my might.

"It's all right, honey. It's all right."

I wondered where I was. I looked around. I was in my room. At home.

"How do I look?"

"You look fine. Tired, but you have been busy with your project."

I jumped out of my bed to race to my dressing table mirror. It was me. I was back, with my dark auburn hair and hazel eyes. The memories of where I had been and what I had done flooded back to me.

"Grandpa, how did I get here?"

"Professor Clawson brought you home. You and that dog you picked up."

He said it so matter-of-factly that it startled me.

"The dog? Plato?"

"Yes, that is what you called him."

"The dog is alive?"

"Yes. What's this about?"

I kept silent, trying to figure it all out for myself.

"Do you know Professor Clawson?"

"Yes, of course."

"How?"

"We worked together on a project, years ago."

"Where's mom and dad?"

"Gone to Philadelphia for the weekend. It's their anniversary. I am supposedly taking care of you."

"What happened?"

"You went to see Professor Clawson. He's helping you with your science project." Grandpa looked concerned. "Ell, why are you confused?"

"I think I overworked myself."

"What exactly is this project?"

"Oh, it's something about time travel."

"Should have known."

"I do go on about it, don't I?

"Professor Clawson wrote a paper on it years ago. He was ridiculed by some, and others found him quite forward thinking. I understand that since his retirement he has a whole new nest of followers."

"Grandpa?"

"Hmm?"

"I am so tired."

"Feel better now, in your stomach? We thought you might have the flu."

"I feel fine. I just need sleep. Lots and lots of sleep."

"The dog needs to come in. He seems quite attached to you. Where did you find him?"

"Oh, in Hamilton. He ran away from someone. I tried to get him to go home." Grandpa looked at me with a big question mark written on his face. "There is something about us, me and the dog. Something, you know, strange."

"Sounds like you have an affinity for one another." Grandpa said it has he walked down the hall to let Plato in.

"What does that mean?"

I heard the clicking of Plato's feet on the hallway floor as he came towards my room. He jumped into my bed, pressed his body against mine, licked my face. I threw my arms around him.

"I have to take better care of you," I said to him.

"He's been fed," grandpa said entering after him. "Affinity means you have one of those magical attractions that no one can explain."

"I see." My eyelids grew heavy.

Grandpa gave me kiss on the forehead, and tucked me in. He patted Plato. When he was gone I got up again to look at myself in the mirror. It was me, yet something was different. It was late, and I needed to sleep. Whatever it was, it would wait until tomorrow. If I had been awake and thinking, I would have asked myself how Plato was still alive. Time travel was weird, and many things were hard to fathom. Sleep was better.

Chapter Eleven

Home for a Spell

I did not return to the warehouse the next day. Nor the day after that. In fact, I lay in bed for three days.

My mother was concerned, thinking me depressed. She queried me but all I would say was that I was tired. Immensely tired.

On the fourth day I got up. I ate breakfast, and then walked to the library. I browsed row upon row of books in the history section. I pressed my fingers across hundreds of titles that covered thousands of years of history. From the glory that was Athens, to the grandeur of Babylon, on to the expansion of Rome, the formation of the various kingdoms of Europe, to the brave men who searched the oceans for new lands and new routes, and on to my own country. The truth is I knew not much about the past. How was I to ride in this fantastic machine the Old Man had invented when I was so ignorant? How arrogant it was of me to travel with others and endanger them!

The librarian knew me well. She looked at me quizzically as I dragged myself to her desk.

"What's the matter Ell?"

"Mrs. Palmer, I think I'm stupid."

"I wouldn't say that. Why do you?"

I sat down in the chair in front of her desk. "I did something stupid."

"What did you do that is so stupid?" Mrs. Palmer leaned her face down to look me directly in the eyes.

"Well, it's like this. I thought I knew more than I do. And things happened that shouldn't have." I looked toward the stack of books. "And then, just now, walking through all those books, I mean, there's so much to know. I want to know history, everything."

"Ell, no one knows *everything*. Not thoroughly. Historians specialize." She paused for a moment in thought. Then she stood. "Come with me."

Mrs. Palmer walked me back to the history section. She took me to the subsection marked "World History."

"This is where you begin. In addition to your school work, you can read these books for an overview of the history of the world. From there, you will find what really appeals to you."

"Like?"

"Well, I am rather found of the Renaissance. To truly understand that era, it's a good idea to learn what led up to it."

"I've heard of the Renaissance."

"Study this first." Mrs. Palmer pulled down a book titled, "The Middle Ages. You cannot understand the Renaissance unless you know what happened during the Middle Ages."

"What about American history?"

She led me to the section on American history. "You've read books on the American War for Independence, now let's move on to study the formation of the Constitution and the first president, Washington. After all, Ell, the formation of the nation took about ten years, but the nation is nearly 200 years old."

"There's a lot to learn."

"Indeed."

By the end of my visit I had checked out four books. I took my stack and then headed home. As I came near the warehouse, I debated whether or not I should stop in to see the professor. It would be rude not to let him know I was well. The office door was open. I stepped in.

"Ell. It's good to see you," the Old Man said as he leaned back in his chair. "Have a seat. Speak to me."

I placed the stack of books on his desk.

"Ah, what do we have here? A book on the Middle Ages, one on Rome, one on the Constitution and here's another one on Rome. Have we inspired you?"

I nodded.

"Are you well? You don't seem your self?"

"I don't think it's me?"

"What's that? What do you mean, 'I don't think it's me'?"

"The thing that happened to me before, when my hair and eyes changed and I could play the piano."

"Are you still playing the piano?"

"We don't have a piano."

"Would you like one?"

This I had to think about. "Perhaps."

"Doesn't sound like there's passion there. Here," he tapped the books, "is your passion, Ell."

I nodded my head.

"But..."

"Yes, but what?"

"When I woke up the other night, I didn't feel right. I couldn't remember anything."

"Ah yes, you had quite the time in your travel. You best speak to Martin about that."

"You know what happened as well as he."

"At this time, we don't know *exactly* what happened. The dog died in 1924 yet he still lives. We don't understand the significance of that, but true, true, something changed. We thought about sending you back to 1777, when the dog first appeared in your timeline. But that, we decided, was too perilous a journey."

We sat in silence for a while, each of us thinking our own thoughts. The Old Man leaned back in his chair, studied the ceiling.

"Time travel, Ell, is risky. It *will* change a person's life in ways we cannot foretell."

"Yes. I can see that now." I picked up the books. "I've come to a decision. As you can see, I want to study more. So I won't be around for a while." I smiled at the professor. How I adored him, and how I would miss the great adventure. He knew that.

"You were too young. I should have known that. Yet you handled yourself so well. Come and see me now and then. Will you?"

"Yes. And tell Martin that I will miss him as well."

The Old Man nodded in agreement. "Take good care of Plato. He's a special dog."

"He is." And then I left.

The years rolled by. From those first four books I learned of Rome and her fall, of Charlemagne and Richard the Lion Heart, of the Crusades, of the plague and the fall of Constantinople. The next four brought me the changes of the late Middle Ages, and how those new ways turned into the Renaissance. When I picked up a book on the Reformation, I went back to the ancients again so that I could get a grounding in philosophy and religion. There were books on the gods of old, books about the Jews and their religion. There were a dozen books on the world of the Christian church and its part in building Western Civilization. There was the rapid rise of Islam, the battles between Islam and Christianity, and between Islam and Islam. Finally, I was ready to read about the discoveries of lands and ideas. The final four gave me America, first as a colony, then as a nation.

A year after I entered high school, my father was offered work in California. We moved. I was loath to give up my friends, but to be on the West Coast was exciting for me. As we packed our belongings, Plato seemed depressed. He moped around the house barely eating anything. The more boxes we piled into the front room, the more he hung his head.

"Don't worry, dogs get worried when they see change," Grandpa said to me.

The movers came on a Monday morning to empty our house. Plato would not leave my side. After the big truck drove away, Plato wagged his tail, sniffed my hand and then bounded out the front door which had been left open. At the moment, I didn't think anything of it. An hour later, he still hadn't returned. I began to worry. When the time came to pile into the car and begin our journey to California, I was gravely worried. Dad drove us around the neighborhood. Plato was no where around, nor had any of our neighbors seen him.

"Honey," Dad said to me, "We have to get going. We will stop off at grandad's and he will continue the search."

Grandpa assured me he would continue looking for Plato until he found him. We then headed west. The thing is, Grandpa never found Plato. I cried over the dog a great deal. Yet, in my heart, I knew he was all right, that he had taken matters into his own hand because he did not want to be in California. Plato, so my gut told me, made his own rules.

My studies in history continued. Every time I ventured on to a new era, I thought of the Old Man. I had neglected him. For what reason I couldn't tell. In my mind, I knew the time would come when I would see him. Would want to see him. My heart would tell me when.

In the third year of high school, I applied to Princeton University. I wanted to go back home to New Jersey. I graduated high school in 1980. In September, I returned to New Jersey. When I had moved into my dorm room, I jumped into my old Jeep and drove to the heart of Trenton to visit the Old Man.

At the warehouse, I knocked on the door, almost afraid that it would be answered and also afraid that it would not. I listened for footsteps. I tried the door. It was open. I walked in finding the office much as it had been except there were more clocks on the wall. Had they always been that noisy, all that ticking going on at once? It was difficult to remember. One chimed, and then the others did. It made me laugh. Would I travel again, with one of those clocks to get me there and back again? I was nearly eighteen now, and in college. Such adventures were time consuming, and dangerous. There were times when I thought I had made the entire thing up in my mind, that I had not really traveled back in time. Yet here was the Old

Man's office with his dozens of clocks to prove I had not made up this place.

The door to the warehouse opened. In came the Old Man carrying one of his clocks, this one made of porcelain formed into flowers painted brightly. He stopped still when he saw me. He had aged a bit, but was still his energetic self.

"Ell," he said. A large smile spread across his face. "Welcome back."

"Hello professor."

"My how you have grown. Why, you are quite pretty."

I blushed.

"Let me put this down." He walked to his desk where he gently laid the clock. "This one is delicate." He came round to me. "Let me look at you. What are you seventeen, eighteen?"

"Eighteen next month."

"Eighteen next month." He shook his head from side to side. "I know from your grandfather that you moved to California."

"Yes. My dad is a construction manager out there for housing projects. They cannot build enough homes it seems."

"And you are going to Princeton."

"Yes."

"Will you major in history?"

"Yes, of course."

"Silly of me to ask the question." He then clapped his hands together. "We have a new chair!"

"A new one?"

He took my hand and led me into the warehouse. There, near where the other chair had been, was a newer one luxuriously upholstered in a cut velvet cloth. This chair was a bit narrower than the other, but the back was taller and the platform around it was wider. This was done because the motor was larger, with more wires running underneath to the panel of controls and dials in front.

"This chair is much more stable than the first."

"You've worked out the kinks?"

"Mostly. But you understand how time travel is. It's not an engineering problem that can be perfected. That doesn't keep us from trying."

"And Martin?"

"I'm not certain where he got off to. The early nineteenth century clock is gone. He could be with Napoleon or Madison."

"Napoleon? Didn't you once tell me the Chair couldn't go over great distances of water?"

"Fixed that."

I sat in the new chair. It was comfortable. I looked over the dials on the dashboard. There were more of them. There were also buttons and switches that the first Chair didn't have.

"Yes," the Old Man said, "it is more complex but that is what gives it its extra stability. We can fine tune."

I fingered the switches. The Old Man watched.

"What do these new switches do?"

"These," he pointed to the ones to my left, "are presets. Think of a place and time you would like to see."

"The opening of the first skyscrapers in Chicago, 1883."

The Old Man began to set the dials. "Let's have you arrive at 2 pm, on the 14th of April, 1883. Now this switch allows you to automatically return without having to set anything else. We put that in to avoid accidents like you had back in 1974."

"And if I want to change the destination?"

"Thinking ahead, are you?" He chuckled. "This switch will allow it, but you must hit it before you try a new programming."

"Here's a red one. What's that one for?

"Ah that. The sad button. If the machine ever needs to be destroyed. Press and then run."

"I see."

"Would you like to take a ride?"

"I don't think so."

He looked disappointed.

"Perhaps later." He said as sat on the stool nearby.

"Perhaps. With my studies, and the activities I'll have at school, I don't think I'll have time for a great, historical adventure." I ran my fingers along the edge of the glass encasement. "I did take those adventures, didn't I?"

"You did." He folded his arms across his chest. "They seem like dreams, do they?" I nodded. "All the more reason to take a small trip."

"I think I had best be going. I need to go see grandpa."

When we had nearly reached the door we heard the familiar sound of the Time Chair. I looked to the new chair. It wasn't going anywhere. The Old Man pushed me inside the office. When the noise and lights of the chair ceased we went back into the warehouse. There, on the old chair, sat Martin. When the glass was up enough, he fell out. He wore the uniform of an early nineteenth century American soldier. He was wounded in his arm. He had lost much blood. I grabbed a towel to wrap his arm in. He looked up at me, a question on his face.

"Ell, that is you, ja?"

Before I could answer he passed out. The two of us dragged him away from the Chair. Just as we did another soldier came tumbling out. This one wore the uniform of a British soldier.

"Oh my, we have the War of 1812 here, professor."

"You have been studying."

"This is an officer." Looking him over, I noted he had a large bump on his head. "Looks like something hit him. Got any ice?"

The professor turned to walk back to the office. He spoke as he did so."He'll need to go back. Preferably before he wakes up." The professor looked straight my way.

"Oh no."

Martin groaned. I pulled the officer out of the chair, looked him over to see what other wounds he might have. The hiss sounded, the glass began to come down again.

"What? Professor!"

The Old Man hurried into the room. He ran to my aide in pulling the soldier out of harms way. Martin came round to crawl away from the chair, but soon collapsed by the table. We turned away as the lights flashed. Seconds later we turned back to see the Chair gone.

"What was that?" the Old Man said as he walked to the empty space. "Martin!"

Martin came round again. "What?"

"Where were you?"

"Take him," Martin pointed to the British officer, "before he discovers where we are and what I am."

Martin seemed delirious.

"That is not what I am asking. The Chair just activated on its own."

No sooner had the words faded away when the lights flashed again.

"It's coming back!" I said.

We all turned away, waiting to hear the familiar noise of the hiss that would signal that it was safe. But instead of that hiss, I heard one of the sweetest sounds ever. A dog's bark. It was muffled at first, but following the hiss, the bark grew steadily louder. I turned to face the machine.

"Plato!"

He jumped out as soon as he could, ran to me and knocked me down. He gave me a thousand dog kisses and I held him tightly in my arms. I laughed, I cried. And I would not let go of him. Whoever or whatever this dog really was, he was *mine*.

"Where have you been, you bad dog," I said amidst my tears. He had no answer except to kiss my face and my hands, and then he curled up to press his body against mine.

"Plato is back," Martin said. "Ja, of course."

"Come on boy, we have work to do." I took the ice pack from the Old Man's hand. I placed it on the officer's head.

"We have to get him back." The Old Man looked me squarely in the face.

"Oh no, not *me*,"

"Ell, I am too old for this. And besides," He glanced at Plato.

"Oh why did I come here?"

The Old Man leaned over to whisper in my ear. "Because you can never give this up. Never."

He was right. I was one of them, forever attracted to the adventure of experiencing history first hand. The Old Man was now really old. Martin was delirious, and needed a doctor's attention. The officer moaned. He was coming to. I ran to the closets to find myself a Regency outfit. In minutes I was dressed. The Old Man helped get the officer into the new chair. I tied on a hat.

"Where am I going?"

"I took the coordinates off the old chair. Looks like you are going back to Baltimore."

"Baltimore? Hear that, Plato. But no Gannon to worry about. Only the British army."

"Pay attention, now Ell. All you need do is hit this button here. When you arrive, drop him off and return immediately." He pointed to a green button near the presets. "The motor is running so hit the green button. And when you want to return, this is all you have to push." He then held out my old pocket watch.

"The same?"

"It too has been improved. Essentially works like it did before, but much more precise." He smiled at me.

I held my hand hovering over the green button.

"Why do I think I will be in grave danger."

"No doubt Ell, you probably will be." He glanced down at the officer. "Nice looking chap. Take good care of him."

"Come on Plato, here we go again."

The dog jumped in and lay on the platform. I hit the green button. The hiss sounded, the glass came down, the motor whined. We were off!

Coming in 2018….

The Time Chair Diary

Book Three

Laura Road

www.ingramcontent.com/pod-product-compliance
Lightning Source LLC
Chambersburg PA
CBHW051512170626
46811CB00002B/780